WE GET LETTERS . . .

"I just finished reading *Star Trek Log One* and loved every single line."

"I very much enjoyed *Star Trek Log One*. It was one of the best screen-to-book adaptations I have read . . ."

"At last a *Star Trek* series that reflects the way I feel about the stories. One that takes the basic situations and characters and builds intelligently on them. I see that you are tying them together—good!"

"Thank you, Mr. Foster, for helping *Star Trek* live!"

"I found your style of writing refreshing and invigorating . . . you supply a large amount of background material which is not explained in the episodes."

"Bravo!"

"You brought out much more than could ever be shown in a half-hour telecast. . . . Keep up the brilliant work."

"I couldn't put the book down once I started it."

"Congratulations . . . Mr. Foster has accurately, tastefully and faithfully reproduced the full flavor of *Star Tr*

"   !"

STAR TREK
LOG THREE

Alan Dean Foster

Based on the Popular Series
Created by GENE RODDENBERRY

BALLANTINE BOOKS • NEW YORK

For Judy-Lynn del Rey

who has the beauty to match her name...

SBN 345-24260-2-125

First Printing: January, 1975
Fifth Printing: July, 1975

Cover art supplied by Filmation Associates

Printed in the United States of America

BALLANTINE BOOKS
A Division of Random House, Inc.
201 East 50th Street, New York, N.Y. 10022
Simultaneously published by
Ballantine Books, Ltd., Toronto, Canada

CONTENTS

PART I

    Once Upon a Planet   1

PART II

    Mudd's Passion   85

PART III

    The Magicks of Megas-Tu   157

STAR TREK LOG THREE

Log of the Starship *Enterprise*

Stardates 5510.1-5524.5 Inclusive

James T. Kirk, Capt., USSC, FS, ret.

Commanding

transcribed by
Alan Dean Foster

At the Galactic Historical Archives
on S. Monicus I
stardated 6111.3

For the curator: JLR

PART I

ONCE
UPON
A PLANET

(Adapted from a script by
Len Janson and Chuck Menville)

1

The officer entered the tent and came unbidden to full attention. For several moments he stood quietly, his eyes never wavering from the tall, impressive figure seated behind the old scarred table. But old campaigner or not, he found himself beginning to fidget. Perhaps his entrance had gone unnoticed. A slight cough as prelude, maybe . . .

"The troops are assembled as you ordered, sir. They're waiting for you."

"Thank you, Centurion," came the warm reply. Caesar did not look up immediately. The battle map sketched out on the tabletop still commanded the full attention of the greatest tactician Rome would ever know.

Their situation was not yet grave, but every hour's delay strengthened the position of the enemy as fresh rebels rallied to their cause.

On the right flank lay the traitor Aranius with his cavalry. To the north Ventrigorix was positioned with the Belgians. A scout had just ridden in with reports of catapults concealed in the high forest to their left that was laden with Greek fire which blackened men and panicked horses.

If their own mounted were dispatched to deal with Aranius' renegades, the thrust of any main assault at the enemy's center would be weakened. Besides, sending even a portion of them to deal with the hidden catapults, whose strength was uncertain, would lessen possibly crucial reserves needed for a decisive conflict. A

3

flank attack would surely follow any center attack, and the entire cavalry would be needed to turn it.

A rising din was heard from outside the tent. Veterans all, the men of the XIIth, XXth, and XXIInd legions had been goaded to a fighting fever by their officers. They were anxious to do battle. To leave them standing while further tactics were deliberated would be folly.

Cries of "Caesar, Caesar!" rose steadily in volume as the troops gave vent to their emotions. The leader of the Roman army thought once more about the vital holocaust ahead.

If this campaign were successful, it would finally break the back of barbarian resistence in northern Gaul. The way would be open to the ice-bound lands across the northern seas, bringing the whole continent under the iron control of Imperial Rome once and for all.

Caesar grinned wolfishly. Then let those limp-wristed Senators and Patricians try to chip away at the Emperor's powers! Rome would see a triumph it would never forget.

Caesar's decision was made even before the fist slammed down onto the table. Eyes rose along with the battle-hardened torso to stare evenly at the tensely waiting centurion.

"Flavius, the moment is at hand. We march!"

Snapping to a position of attention the centurion's right arm shot up and out in salute. The words he had been waiting for—the words three legions of Rome's finest troops had been waiting for.

"Hail, Caesar," he intoned admiringly. "Your legions await your command."

And this was more than rhetoric, for by now the tent was all but swaying to the combined shouts of thousands of massed soldiers.

Donning his helmet, Caesar buckled on the short

sword, adjusted a chinstrap, and strode toward the waiting thunder to address her men . . .

"What's the matter with you, Yeoman?" asked a worried Lt. Davis. "Haven't you got that stand-by program for the menu worked out yet?"

Yeoman Deb Colotti blinked and looked up from her dream.

"What . . . ? Sorry, Lieutenant. My . . . my mind was floating."

"That's because it's lighter than air," snapped the section chief. She glanced over Colotti's shoulder and tapped a finger on the bright digital readout.

"Code SCRP-D-220. You've just programed two hundred and twenty chocolate raisin pies into the month's menu. And the captain hates chocolate raisin pie. Get busy and fix it."

"Yes, ma'am." Colotti shook her head at her own idiocy and started in on the tedious task of erasing and resetting the faulty program she had just fed into the *Enterprise*'s galley computer.

Dry leaves crackled like brown foil underfoot and N'gombi froze. Behind him, the other four men of the hunting party did likewise, becoming as motionless as the surrounding trees of the great rain forest. Much care was necessary here, on the very edge of the veldt. Only anxious eyes continued to move, searching, probing nervously into the surrounding wall of green.

The hunting party remained frozen in place several minutes longer before moving forward again. Almost immediately N'gombi threw up a warning hand. A clear section of soft, rain-soaked earth lay in front of them. Kneeling, he examined the track left in the drying mud.

A sniff, loose earth crumbled appraisingly between sensitive fingers. "Fresh . . . very fresh," he muttered.

His senses wholly alert, N'gombi looked up and into

the forest. The spoor was barely minutes old. Behind him he could feel the tenseness of the others as they waited for his words.

All were brave men—the bravest of the village. But they had no stomach for this kind of work and none could blame them. Especially in dense undergrowth where a group had no room to spread out and maneuver, where death could sneak smell-close to strike and crush and rend before a man could turn to see.

Only the willingness of the great slayer N'gombi had given them enough courage, enough to go too. But even with the quiet assured presence of their greatest hunter, the sudden absence of normal jungle sounds—the monkey cries and the shrieking of brilliant-plumed parrots—was frightening them.

N'gombi rose and started to step over the track. As he did so, a frightening crashing sounded in the foliage to their left. For a moment the party held. Then, screaming in fear and sudden panic, the other four hunters dropped their spears and ran for their lives retreating back down the path.

Turning quietly, N'gombi grounded his spear-butt firmly into the dirt, knelt on one knee, and braced the hardwood shaft . . . and waited.

Like a falling sandstone cliff, the tawny form of the huge rogue lion exploded out of the brush and at him . . .

Subengineer Duchamps shouldered his overchalked cue and stared curiously across the green-felt-covered table.

"You're not on your game today, Henry. That's the fourth round of eight-ball I've taken from you this morning."

"Yeah," agreed security guard Henry Ndugu, observing idly that his partner had indeed swept the table surface clean. "Guess I can't concentrate."

"Don't wonder why," nodded Duchamps knowingly.

He glanced at the chronometer on his wrist as he swung the cue free. "Must be only a couple of hours out by now." He sighed deeply.

"I'm having a hard time keeping my attention on the game, too. But I figure I might as well fulfill at least one fantasy right now. It's nice to beat you for a change. Rack 'em up . . ."

In the pilot house, Captain Benjamin O. Lee puffed nervously on his pipe and glanced out of the corner of an eye at his pilot. Strange sort of chap, this pilot, giving up a promising literary career just to come back to his home town and sign on with a dirty old steamboat.

But the fellow seemed steady enough. Lee was damned happy to have him. Had the surest eyes and steadiest hands on the river.

It was a quiet summer day. Just enough of a breeze wafted over the river to keep the humidity from killing. From the iron stacks, gritty black smoke seemed to rise vertically into otherwise azure sky. The *Cairo* was entering a sharp bend in the channel.

Noticing the direction of the captain's eyes, the pilot smiled that funny, wry smile of his. "Don't worry, Cap'n. We'll get through easy as my grandfather's old ram."

"I sure hope so, Sam. Never seen the big muddy this low. If those folks at Paducah don't get these medical supplies and that new vaccine we've got on B-deck, well . . ." His eyes lowered.

"Now I told you not to worry, Cap'n. I know every log, every sandbar and old wreck this river's ever belched up. She's never played me false yet, and I don't see her doin' it now. Even so," and he eyed the swirling, muddy water ahead where a narrow stream entered the main course, "it'd be good to take a sounding about here."

The captain nodded. Something at least to take his

mind off less happy thoughts. Leaning out the side window of the pilot house he shouted forward.

"Mr. Hansen . . . take a sounding!"

"Aye, Cap'n!" came the mate's reply. The Swede uncoiled the measured, weighted line and chucked it easily over the bow, slightly to port. He checked the line markings as the paddle-wheeler pushed steadily ahead.

"Mark Twain!" he called back toward the bridge. The pilot nodded and turned the wheel slightly to starboard. His eyes, perpetually twinkling under bushy brows, looked skyward. If the weather held they'd make Paducah in plenty of time . . .

"Not much point in letting a recorder run if you're not going to use it," observed Yeoman Lancer.

Ensign Ub Jackson started, looked up, suddenly aware that the screen in front of him was illuminated but quite blank, patiently awaiting instructions.

"Sorry, Lily. Seems I just can't turn out any poetry today."

"What's the matter?" She checked the list of suggestive titles available on another unoccupied viewer, and resolutely turned away from it. Best save her fantasies for the real thing. "No inspiration?"

By way of answer Jackson activated the recorder. But instead of slipping in a program cassette, he dialed the image currently displayed on the main viewscreen up on the bridge.

The screen fluttered momentarily, then cleared to reveal a blue-white world draped in a delicate peignoir of clouds. It had grown visibly since the last time he had looked at it.

"No," he finally replied, eyeing the approaching planet longingly, "too much of it."

"Captain's Log, stardate 5510.1," Kirk informed the patient pickup at his wrist. He paused, glancing around the quietly efficient bridge. Spock, Uhura, Sulu, and Arex were occupied preparing for orbital insertion, each at his respective station. Dr. McCoy stood at Arex's shoulder, peering past the helmsman at their destination.

"The crew of the *Enterprise*," he continued, satisfied that everything and everyone was operating normally, "is ready for some well-deserved rest and recreation. And the sooner the better. Mr. Spock informs me that normal ship efficiency is down twenty-two percent from the standard level—due in part to anticipation of Omicron planetfall."

That was an understatement. Ship's personnel were so involved in plotting out the elaborate fantasies they hoped to enjoy once down on the surface of that azure ceramic world that only automatic instrumentation kept the *Enterprise* in working order.

"Having secured the situation on Phylos and submitted the information concerning the mutant clone Stavos Keniclius V and mutant Spock Two—clone of our own first officer—to Starfleet sector headquarters, I requested that the crew be granted something special in the way of shore leave. Said request to visit the Omicron region was duly submitted and approved.

"Course was set and traced without incident. We are now approaching that so-called 'shore-leave' world.

"Those studying this log may recall that this particular planet was programed long ago by some unknown but highly advanced alien race. The extremely complex machinery installed there is designed solely to provide fun and amusement for interstellar passersby.

"Its extensive mind-reading devices and attendant manufacturing machinery are capable of materializing any fantasy they can pick up. I confess to looking forward to our return to this planet myself."

Switching off the recorder Kirk sat back and watched his fellow officers at work. Although they betrayed no

outward emotion, Kirk was certain they shared the
same feelings of expectation he did.

As he stared at the earthlike globe floating in the
center of the main viewscreen, his mind relaxed for the
first time in weeks. At last they would have a real rest,
unencumbered by requests to explore, aid, fight, or otherwise exercise themselves on behalf of Federation pol-
icy.

Matter of fact, a little anticipatory daydreaming
wouldn't hurt right now . . .

The *Enterprise* was run on three eight-hour shifts.
Her crew would take a shore leave the same way. A
games computer served to scramble a complete roster of
personnel and then print out one lucky third of them.

Uhura, Sulu, and McCoy were all in the first group
scheduled for beam down. McCoy in particular made
no effort to hide his pleasure in being among the first of
the ship's complement permitted to sample the dream-
satisfying pleasures ahead.

The outcome did not sit very well with Engineer
Scott, however. He looked up disapprovingly from his
station behind the transporter console.

"You needn't look so smug about it, Doctor."

"Now, Scotty, no need to be jealous. You're due to
beam down with the next group anyway, aren't you?"

Scott shook his head mournfully. "Uh-uh . . . I'm in
the third shift."

"Too bad. Well, we'll try not to use up the planet."
He grinned and followed Uhura and Sulu into the
transporter alcove.

Scott started to activate the transporter controls but
paused at the sight of a familiar object slung over
Sulu's right shoulder. He stared at it curiously. "This is
supposed to be a pleasure stop, Lieutenant Sulu. Why
the science tricorder?"

"I thought you knew, Chief. Botany's one of my
hobbies. Oh, you can't be sure about much of anything
down there, but lots of the plants are native. And the

planetary computer's had the green thoughts of thousands of alien visitors to draw on to grow others. Not everybody's fantasies are lurid garden-of-eden types. Mine's just plain gardens."

Scott shrugged. "Each to his own, I suppose. Seems like a bit of a waste to me, though." His voice assumed a conspiratorial tone. "Now, when my turn comes I plan to . . ."

"If you don't mind I'd really rather do without the juicy details, Chief," Uhura interrupted sharply. "We've all got our own dreams to indulge, and we can't do it standing here."

"Ummmm, is that a subtle hint, lass?" Scott smiled wickedly. "Sorry." He activated three levers, twirled switches and knobs. The three officers, complete with separate fantasies, turned into three multicolored pillars of shifting particles.

These reformed later, touching down amid a landscape of ethereal beauty. This particular section of the planet had been planted and tossed and sculpted and rearranged to look like a Bierstadt canvas. Foliage here had been groomed by the touch of a master stylist. Thick grassy meadows and small brooks alternated as far as one could see. Miniature waterfalls lifted from Japanese prints (or the memory of same) provided delicately orchestrated background music. Here and there trees blended harmoniously into the meadows, trees grown as much for symmetry as for shade. Some were draped loosely with climbing vines that were festooned in turn with blooms of gold, green, and tyrolean purple. In the distance, part-way up a gradual slope, they saw a vibrating, glittering flash of color. Another landing party beaming down. Even further away, on the other side of a gentle river, yet a third group arrived. Flashes continued intermittently at a rapidly increasing range as the *Enterprise*'s transporters freckled the surface with landing parties of would-be lotus-eaters.

McCoy took a few experimental steps, turning in a slow circle to take in views of the high, snow-capped mountains that surrounded this valley. Were those distant peaks the result of natural upheaval—or were they planned on some master map by contouring computers buried deep beneath their feet? There was no way to tell.

At the foot of the mountains ran a long, clear lake, positioned like a mirror to best reflect the towering crags and pinnacles. It, at least, looked too perfect to be anything but the result of some other geologically inclined traveler's idealized dreamscape.

McCoy nodded to himself, completely satisfied. "Just as gorgeous as I remember it. Doesn't look like anything's changed, not a leaf, not a blade of grass."

They started walking toward the nearest little stream. It bubbled capriciously down a hillside that looked misty where there was no mist. That puzzled Sulu. He'd seen this slope before somewhere. But where?

In a painting, of course, and the image came to him abruptly. This hillside, those trees and rockfalls, the stream, had been designed once before, by a long-dead terran artist . . . Masefield . . . no, Maxfield Parrish.

Seeing it in all three dimensions was startling.

"This looks a lot like the same spot we set down at on our first visit," he ventured. Then the helmsman smiled, recalling a fantasy other than his own.

"Remember when we saw the white rabbit, Doctor?"

McCoy chuckled before replying. "It's not the sort of thing you forget. Sure I remember, Sulu. And all because I said this place made me feel like a character out of *Alice in Wonderland.*"

Suddenly they were unexpectedly interrupted. It wasn't quite a human voice, but more like a caricature of one. A high piping wail that was half-child, half-senator.

"One side, one side!"

McCoy spun around and barely cleared the path in

time as a meter-tall white rabbit clad in top hat and tails bounded past. The rabbit was holding onto his bobbing hat with one hand and clutching tightly to an oversized gold pocket watch with the other. His manner and tone were agitated, his bouncy stride hurried.

"I'm late, I'm late! Oh my fuzzy ears and whiskers, I'm very very late!"

Repetition of a previous incident or not, Sulu, McCoy, and Uhura stood gaping at the furry apparition as it shot past. The rabbit unexpectedly left the path and, with a hop of Olympian proportions, sailed into the thick shrubbery.

Moments later, naturally, a young girl emerged seemingly from nowhere on the path in front of them. She had long blond hair neatly combed to her waist, and she wore a light blue dress with matching white pinafore, knee-high socks, and shiny black buckled shoes.

By the time she had come close enough to tap Uhura on the shoulder, they'd all recovered from the initial surprise.

"I beg your pardon," the girl said politely in a thick British-terran accent, "but did you happen to see a large white rabbit come this way?"

Uhura pointed toward the concealing bushes. "He went that way, Alice."

"Thank you so much!" She performed a perfect little curtsey and hurried off down the path, disappearing into the same bushes as the rabbit. Sulu and McCoy exhanged charmed smiles.

"Just like you said, Doctor, nothing's changed."

Uhura smiled agreement, then shook her head in wonderment. "They're such perfect models, so exact— and they appear so quickly in response to your thoughts. It's hard to believe they're not real."

"Easy, Lieutenant," cautioned McCoy, but gently. "They're only highly sophisticated robots, whipped up by this world's central computer to make your dreams come true."

"I know," she responded. "I wish I could have a look at their insides. Imagine the technology required to direct and guide them, without any sign of receiving or transmitting apparatus. Nothing in the Federation comes close to it." She paused at a sudden thought, and Sulu and McCoy stopped to watch her.

"I wish," she began, spacing her words deliberately, "I could see their insides, especially the transmit-receive instrumentation." They waited, but the hidden ears of the planet chose not to give a response.

"I said," she repeated firmly, "I *wish* to see the insides of one of the automatons."

Sulu shook his head. "Forget it, Uhura. But it was a nice idea." She smiled ruefully back at him.

"I guess granting your heart's desire doesn't include giving away trade secrets. The planetary machinery will do just about anything, except explain itself. Oh well." She shrugged philosophically, then smiled.

"This won't do—acting disappointed. Got to think only happy thoughts."

"My prescription exactly," McCoy agreed. "Speaking of which . . ." He looked slightly embarrassed. "Part of the pleasure of being on this world is indulging in your most private fantasies, to the hilt. That requires a certain amount of, uh . . ."

"Privacy," supplied Sulu. "Just what I was going to say."

"And I," Uhura added, making it unanimous.

"Not that I'm not crazy about both of you," the good doctor retorted hastily, "but when I see you again I'd just as soon we were back on the ship."

The three starship officers split up amiably then, taking off in three different directions, searching out three different paths through the manicured lawns—each in search of a place where secret dreams could be enjoyed away from the rest of humanity.

Exotic blossoms bordered the bubbling rivulet, petals straining so hard to catch the sun that some bloomed even under the clear surface of the stream. They existed nowhere else in the universe, having been cultivated and grown first in the field of the mind.

A faint tinge of rose tinted the otherwise diamond-clear water, and thick clover sighed with the action of wind on a billion waiting stems. The scene required only its creator for completeness.

Uhura furnished that seconds later as she topped the rise that concealed the perfect valley and then started down toward the stream.

She stared down, down, into the water. A wavering rippled reflection of self looked back at her. Reaching out, the reflection grasped the water-distorted mirror-image of a large black flower and plucked it free, setting it into the hair above one ear. Then it smiled up at Uhura.

Humming softly, she imitated the suggestive action of her reflection. Breaking off the self-same flower she set it neatly over the indicated ear. Still humming softly to herself, she started to stroll upstream.

Immense was the forest, with gnarled trees impossibly thick and tall. Like bark-backed skyscrapers they soared hundreds of meters into the sky. Their distant crests seemed to support the blue heavens on thick, brown branches.

Sulu rounded one colossal bole and leaned to study the moss growing on its side. Here the wood was the shade of obsidian, the iron-hard black fluted and ribboned with channels, the touch smooth as oiled ivory. Yet when he pressed in, the black bark gave way obediantly.

Delicate dark vines encircled many of the towering trees. They dangled freely from the lowest branches.

Each was composed of segments, like a chain. When a lithe breeze gusted, the links would bounce against one another, tinkling with a sound of small porcelain chimes. It was the only sound in the forest.

Light shafted down in yellow ranks between the trunks, and the effect was like walking through a cathedral. Transparent flowers grew here and there from high bushes. Whenever they caught the light they made presents of rainbows to the helmsman's delighted eyes. The rest of the undergrowth was riotous, wild, every bit as impressive in its own way as the massive trees.

Once, a tiny fuzzy plant pulled itself out of the ground and started to follow him, scurrying along in pursuit on tiny mobile roots. Sulu grinned at the memory that had produced it. Then he bent, lifted it easily in one hand. Tiny thorns pricked futilely at his palm. Bringing both hands together, he slowly ground the fuzzy into a handful of yellow powder.

One puff was sufficient to send the dust floating away. Sulu rubbed his hands together as he continued through the forest. A lilting tune came unbidden to his lips. His singing voice might not have been good, but it was enthusiastic, and the chiming vines seemed to join right in.

Thick twisted cypress alternated politely with slim, zebra-striped birch. Like the hair of a goddess, Spanish moss fell in emerald waves from the thicker trees, almost touching the ground. Somewhere an oriole chirped a greeting as McCoy turned a bend in the lane. He stopped to absorb the view.

Ahead, set on a low hill surrounded by well-tended green lawns and a newly painted white picket fence, was a magnificent cream-colored mansion. It was two-stories high and faced with smooth, pseudoclassical columns. Honeysuckle, wisteria, and magnolia bloomed in profusion around the front gate. The flowers tangled around the fence and climbed up the fronting columns, alternating with thick ivy and filling the air with scents of sugar and sweet wine. Somewhere, someone was plunking a banjo and singing.

McCoy sighed and stared longingly at the distant panorama, resolutely putting out of his mind the fact that the front was probably false, the ivy artificial, and the banjo-plucker a hidden recording.

"Lovely . . . they just don't make 'em like that anymore." He started toward the mansion and was wondering who would greet him at the door, when a harsh female voice shattered the antebellum tranquillity.

"Off with his head!"

McCoy spun around in surprise. What greeted him was no less unlikely but a good deal more startling than the plantation now behind him. A large crowd of oddly shaped humanoids returned his stare. Their gaze was openly hostile.

Each body was a perfect rectangle save only for five bulges—head, arms, and legs. Their torsos were tremendously broad, impossibly thin, and inscribed with archaic symbols: hearts, diamonds, spades, and clubs.

The unmistakable leader of this angry horde was somewhat less broad and rather less narrow. She stepped out of their midst and jabbed an accusing finger at McCoy.

"There he is!" she shrieked. "Off with his head!"

Lowering their lances, the card-shaped humanoids charged forward on stumpy legs.

It was all a dazed McCoy could do to duck just as a lance tipped with a razor-edged heart sailed over his head, cutting a small sapling behind him neatly in half. It suddenly occurred to the *Enterprise*'s chief physician that the intentions of this multiple fantasy were other than benign.

"Hey, what's going on here?" Something brushed his right arm and slammed into the large tree behind. This one was finished with a dark spade-shape, half of which was buried in the wood. McCoy glanced down at his side, saw that the spear had taken a neat slice out of his tunic. That did it. He had no intention of hanging around to argue with a belligerent dream, especially when it wasn't his. He turned and took off down the path on the dead run.

"Stop him!" yelled the Queen. The cards had already taken off in hot pursuit, and the pack of humanoids was close on McCoy's heels.

Occasionally a long lance arched through the air near him. Fortunately the aim of his pursuers was not good. Their short arms did not permit much in the way of long-range accuracy. McCoy had no intention of giving them a chance to sharpen their skills at close range. With his longer legs McCoy was able to maintain and even slightly lengthen his lead. But he was no athlete and he couldn't keep up this chase indefinitely, whereas the animated cards could probably run all day.

Fumbling at his belt he finally managed to pull the communicator free. It took him three frantic tries before the cover snapped back, but by then he was panting so hard that the words refused to form.

Finally, however, he managed to gasp between breaths, "*Enterprise*—emergency, emergency! Beam up, beam up!"

The filtered shouts sounded clearly over the speaker in the transporter room. Fortunately Scott was on station there, alert for just such a call. Not that the chief engineer had suddenly acquired the gift of precognition. It was standard procedure, ever since the amazing properties of the shore-leave world had become known, to have someone standing by at the transporter at all times. Some crewmembers got bored early and had to be beamed back before their rest time was expired.

But the real reason for the precaution was that one or two members of a ship's complement often could not handle the confrontation with their own fantasies. Though they were in no danger of physical harm, a real chance of serious mental damage existed unless they could be brought back aboard in time.

But this sounded like McCoy—one of the last people Scott expected to have to bring back early. He didn't sound bored, and if one person on the *Enterprise* was well qualified to handle his own fantasies, it was the ship's head medical officer.

Still, there was no arguing with that emergency call. McCoy had apparently not strayed far from the original set-down point—he had hardly had time—and Scott located him quickly. Then a hand was moving on one of the controlling levers.

McCoy, panting heavily, dodged around a thick oak. An improbable, scythe-headed lance shot through the space he had occupied a moment before. He looked over his shoulder. They had gotten behind him somehow, and now a handful of the cards were moving toward him.

Desperately McCoy searched for a way out, took a step sideways. If he could make the stream—there was always a chance the cards hadn't been programed to swim. Then he started to scream.

A hurled lance was coming straight at his face.

It reached him.

II

Uhura blinked and stared at her own communicator as if it had suddenly started talking to her with a mind of its own. She had been preparing to call in and make certain all was well with Lt. M'ress in communications, when the sound of McCoy's emergency call had been relayed automatically to her over the open channel.

She paused by a small waterfall. What could there be on this paradise world to menace anyone? Despite the obvious urgency of McCoy's call, her attention stayed divided between the communicator and the liquid jewel set into the hillside.

"Uhura to transporter room, come in, please." M'ress could wait. First she ought to find out what was the trouble with McCoy.

In one instant the scene was normal, complete. Grass, her hand, the communicator, tiny flowers at her feet. Then a long metal shape inserted itself into her view. Taking the communicator effortlessly from her grasp, it closed pewter-toned digits. There was an ugly crackling sound, and the tough device was pulverized into tiny fragments of metal and mangled components.

She turned and gave a little gasp of surprise.

The hovercraft was not very big. Just about a meter high and long, it floated off the ground quite close to her. It sported six mechanical arms of varying length. Each was equipped with different nodes and knobs at its end. The function of five of them remained a mystery. The sixth had been used to crush the communicator.

Electronic lenses—light sensors or true artificial eyes,

she couldn't tell which—ringed the efficient-looking machine. So far it hadn't threatened her, hadn't moved at all except to destroy the communicator.

She took a couple of uncertain steps away from it. The muted hum the automaton generated rose slightly in pitch, and it moved to follow her, a silent steel-eyed spider.

Kirk lolled in the command chair and glared at the main viewscreen. At the moment it displayed a vivid rectangular field of nothing. And he worried. Spock sat nearby, while Arex sat at the navigation console and tried to look busy. M'ress rested at the communications station and nervously ran her claws across the metal board in front of her.

Finally the elevator opened, and McCoy and Sulu hurried in. Kirk swiveled. He noticed the doctor's torn sleeve immediately. It was a neat cut, and you didn't have to be a botanist to see that it hadn't been produced by any interfering branch.

"What happened down there, Bones?"

McCoy was clearly bewildered and making no attempt to conceal the fact. "I can't understand it, Jim. Everything looked exactly the same as last time. It behaved exactly as last time. We even met Alice and the White Rabbit again.

"So we split up, each to his own fantasy-world. Everything proceeded beautifully—for Sulu and me, at least." That triggered another thought, and the doctor glanced around the bridge. "Say, where is Uhura, anyway?"

"Hasn't come back yet," supplied Kirk helpfully, "but we haven't received any emergency call from her, nor from any of the other shore parties. Lt. Sulu just happened to have come back on his own, to drop off his specimens and get a bigger collecting pouch. Go on."

"Everything was happening just as I wished it

would, when suddenly this army of animated playing cards appeared out of nowhere. Only they weren't playing." He fingered his torn sleeve.

"I nearly got aced, Jim." Nobody smiled.

"Animated cards?" The doctor nodded.

"Led by the Queen of Hearts herself."

"The Queen of Hearts and her army of cards are characters from *Alice Through the Looking Glass*, Captain," Spock informed him.

"I just remembered myself, Spock. I read the book as a child. But I wasn't aware that you were attracted to the literature of the fantastic. I thought general and hard science was more your style."

"Light reading is considered relaxing, as well as mentally healthful," the first officer replied. "My mother was particularly fond of Lewis Carroll's work." He looked thoughtful. "Considering the realities of life on Vulcan, it is not surprising that a good deal of her reading tended to the opposite extreme."

"I understand." Kirk turned back to confront McCoy. "Bones, you said you'd already entered your own fantasy of the moment. You weren't thinking about that book?"

"Absolutely not! As a matter of fact, I distinctly recall thinking how beautiful and peaceful and right everything was. And then before you know it, it's 'Off with his head!' *My* head." He added by way of rapid afterthought, "No comments from you, Spock."

Spock protested mildly. "I was not about to say anything, Doctor."

"Mr. Sulu," Kirk continued, shifting his attention to the helmsman, "did you experience anything out of the ordinary—that is, anything out of the ordinary you didn't wish for? Was there anything in your fantasy that either didn't belong there, or acted antagonistically?"

"No, sir. The contrary, if anything."

"Well then—" Kirk halted in midsentence as Scott's voice sounded over the open communicators.

"Transporter room to Captain Kirk." He thumbed the respond switch.

"Kirk here. What is it, Scotty?"

"Captain, contact has been lost with Lieutenant Uhura. I can't get a fix on her anywhere. She's still down on the surface, but the monitor signal from her communicator has disappeared."

"Sensor scan, Mr. Spock," Kirk said curtly.

"Yes, Captain." Spock turned his eyes and attention to his hooded viewer, began working controls. Kirk turned back and spoke into the pickup.

"Scotty, retrieve all landing parties immediately. All leaves are cancelled."

"Aye, Cap'n. But what'll I tell the rest of the crew?" The chief engineer sounded concerned. "Some of the second shift are already pressin' me to slip them down a few minutes earlier."

"You can tell them there's an emergency, Scotty," Kirk suggested, "but don't specify its nature. If anyone presses you for details, tell them it doesn't seem to be serious."

Scott didn't reply immediately, and Kirk could visualize the chief engineer's face, a mask of hesitation. He didn't believe in white lies anymore than in white rabbits. But Kirk knew the chief would see his way toward rationalizing the situation. They didn't know that Uhura was in any trouble; they only knew that her signal had gone out. It might be a mechanical malfunction.

"All right, Cap'n," came the reply.

"And keep trying to locate her. We'll be working on it from this end."

"Aye, sir. Scott out." Kirk clicked off, swung to look over at Spock.

"Any data yet, Mr. Spock?"

"Nothing, Captain. According to all sensor scans,

there is no evidence to show that Lieutenant Uhura is even in the general beam-down area."

Kirk drummed thoughtful fingers on the arm of the command chair. A sudden thought, and he glanced back at the watching figures of Sulu and McCoy.

"She's still got to be there, under cover of some kind."

"Then you don't believe it's a mechanical breakdown, Jim?"

"No, Bones. Communicator breakdown is one thing, but that doesn't explain why Spock's sensors can't pick up her pattern. What I don't understand is why the Keeper of the planet hasn't put in an appearance. I'd be a lot less worried about Uhura if he'd come to your aid, Bones."

"That's right," McCoy exclaimed. "He's supposed to make sure that no one is injured by the fantasy-fulfilling mechanisms." Ruefully he fingered his sleeve above the tear, where the lance had grazed him.

"I didn't see him either," offered Sulu.

"I can only guess he didn't want us to see him," McCoy assumed. "Something's very wrong down there, all right. He should have shown up the minute those crazy cards came after me."

"Aren't his headquarters supposed to be somewhere underground?" asked Kirk.

"Presumably they would be adjacent to the central computer, which is responsible for operating and directing the wish-replying programs," Spock hypothesized.

"Do we have any idea where that might be, Spock?" The science officer shook his head.

"We know that there are a multitude of major centers producing and servicing the fantasy machinery. According to readings obtained on previous visits to the planet, these centers are shielded by a unique combination of restructured granite and metallic alloys.

"Our sensors will not penetrate this peculiar material. Therefore we have no way of determining which of numerous underground centers is the central control area itself. We can only speculate."

Kirk mused a moment longer. Then he was giving out instructions even as he rose from the chair.

"Mr. Arex, you have the conn." The navigation officer nodded, and command passed as smoothly as that. "There will be an immediate investigating party beamed down—said group to consist of Spock, Sulu, Dr. McCoy, and myself. No one else is to beam down to the surface even for a moment unless authorized by direct order from me. Is that clear, Lieutenant?"

"Yes sir," Arex responded. M'ress hissed angrily, hoping nothing had happened to her close friend Uhura.

Her reflection in the stream was blurred by the current, blurred and distorted. Slowly the ripples stirred, tumbled; she felt queasy. Then the reflections suddenly stilled and became smooth again. Uhura shook her head dizzily, slowly becoming aware that the ripples had been in her head and not in the stream. Strong light flooded the room.

Room—that wasn't right. She was outside, by the magic brook. But the nightmare had come and . . .

Abruptly she was fully conscious.

The underground complex in which she found herself was not endless: it merely seemed that way. Row on row of computer components and intricate machinery stretched as far as the eye could see. Directly in front of her was an alien, oddly shaped console fronted with an assortment of glowing display screens. One central screen dominated the others out of sheer size. It was much bigger than the main viewscreen on the bridge of the *Enterprise*.

"What's going on?" she said, in sheer reflex. "Why have I been brought here?"

A mild, rolling voice issued from the central region of the console, and she took a step backward. The voice was thoroughly mechanical. No organic force spoke through that hidden speaker.

"You are being detained," the voice said, "so that your master will not leave."

Captain she would have understood, or superior, or leader, but: "My master?"

The voice deigned to elaborate. "The skymachine."

Uhura thought furiously. This was a lot more confusing than the simple appearance of Alice and the White Rabbit. Taken in conjunction with her abduction and the emergency call she had heard over the communicator, that statement assumed threatening proportions.

"Skymachine? Explain yourself."

"Your intelligence quotient is apparently lower than I had initially assessed. I refer to the skymachine which enslaves you. The skymachine now in orbit around my world."

"You mean the *Enterprise*?" If the machine could interpret vocal inflection, it would have no trouble detecting her honest confusion.

"I believe that is your name for it." A pause, then, "Yes, I see that it is."

"But—" No, she'd need more information on which to found an argument. No telling how the thought processes of this clearly crazed machine were working.

"Why do you think the *Enterprise* is my . . . my master?"

"That question is redundant. It appears that I must again revise my initial estimates of your intelligence downward."

Now Uhura was angry as well as confused. "Then I'll make a statement you won't find quite so redundant. If I'm not released immediately, my fellow crewmembers will come looking for me. I don't think you'll like the results if they find you."

This did not produce the half hoped-for outburst of electronic contrition. Instead, the computer voice replied calmly, "They are already here."

The viewscreen set in the face of the wall-high console came on. Uhura moved slightly nearer, keeping a wary eye to one side. A pair of the six-legged hovercraft servitors floated nearby, watching her.

Light darkened, rolled, and cleared on the screen, to reveal a clear view of Spock, Sulu, Kirk, and McCoy walking somewhere on the surface. The image was breathtakingly perfect, so much so that she had to resist an urge to reach out and grab Kirk's arm.

"Unfortunately, much as I abhor material waste," the voice continued indifferently, "I have no use for more than one hostage. This leaves me no choice but to turn them off."

To confusion and anger was now added fear. "Turn them off?"

"Again you persist in redundancy. No, I see that you do not comprehend. I will make them ... cease to function."

"Cease to ... you mean, kill them—no, put them to sleep, you mean, like you did when you brought me down here."

"The first word," queried the computer, "that is a term which means 'cease to function?' "

"Yes, but—"

"Then it appears communications are sufficient after all." The voice sounded satisfied. "It is as I wish; I will turn them off."

Kirk was grumbling irritably and trying to look twelve directions at once. "We travel all this way, cross parsecs, wanting nothing more than a little rest and take-it-easy time. Instead, you get attacked by a fantasy of unknown origin, Bones, and now Uhura is missing."

There was a beep from the communicator hooked to his belt. He flipped it open. "Kirk here."

"Lieutenant Arex, sir," came the distant voice of the navigation officer. "We've completed the total sensor scan of the surface. No sign of Lieutenant Uhura."

"Thank you, Mr. Arex. Keep sensors active in our immediate area and let me know the minute anything interesting happens. Kirk out."

"She must be in the underground system," Sulu insisted grimly. "There's no way she could have been taken off-planet without being detected."

"There's one other possibility," McCoy observed. "Sensors wouldn't pick her up on the surface if she were dead."

It was quiet for long moments. "We could save a lot of time," Kirk mused, breaking the silence, "if we could locate the Keeper." He looked understandably frustrated. "I still can't understand why he didn't intervene when you were attacked, Bones."

"I'd like to know the reason, myself, Jim."

Spock halted and held his tricorder out in front of him, sensors aimed groundward. A moment later he confirmed what they already knew.

"Instruments indicate the presence of a shielding barrier of restructured natural material combined with metals, Captain."

Kirk dropped to one knee and dug at the soft loam. The short, thick-looking grass came up with surprising ease. Several centimeters below the last roots his fingers encountered something that didn't crumble.

A few minutes later, he and Sulu had cleared a circle about a half meter in diameter. Below the dirt lay a seamless layer of oddly shiny rock, whitish-gray in the bright sunlight.

It was exactly what they expected, but that didn't prevent Kirk from rising and throwing a handful of dirt angrily aside. "This world is built like a fortress."

"If that's really the material Spock says it is, Captain," observed Sulu.

"I do not follow, Mr. Sulu," confessed Spock.

Sulu grinned mirthlessly. "Simple, Spock. This planetary master computer whatsis is a master of illusion. It might be able to fool your tricorder into reading an impenetrable barrier where there's nothing but plain old rocks."

Kirk grunted. "We'll find out how much of it is real and how much is fortress fantasy in a few minutes. The phaser bore can cut through twenty meters of any kind of stone in seconds. This stuff may be tougher—we may need minutes. But cut through it we will." He flipped open the communicator again.

"Kirk to *Enterprise*."

Lt. M'ress's voice responded instantly.

"*Enterprise*, Captain."

"Lieutenant, have Mr. Scott beam down the phaser bore and—" There was a sharp, crinkling sound as a burst of static drowned out his transmission. "*Enterprise*, do you read me?"

M'ress's voice replied, but it was weak, barely intelligible, and had to fight its way through a steadily mounting haze of interference.

"Your signals are growing weaker, sir," came the communications officer's fading voice. Further words followed, swallowed by static, then, "Suggest you repeat . . ."

That was the last coherent word they received. Try as he might, Kirk was unable to reestablish contact with the ship. Nor did any of the other officers have any better luck with their communicators. Every band was submerged under a tidal wave of sudden interference.

There was always the outside chance that the trouble was the communicators themselves, but it was hardly likely. Spock confirmed Kirk's fears a moment later.

He had removed the back of the tiny transmitter, adjusted his tricorder, and used the latter instrument to evaluate the condition of the first. Now he clipped the protective plate back onto the communicator and looked around at the waiting circle.

"They're definitely not malfuctioning, Captain. We

have been cut off by the imposition of an artificial electronic block."

"Let's wait a few minutes, anyway," Kirk suggested. "There's a chance, judging from M'ress's reaction, that the important part of the message got through."

Scott asked her one more time. "You're sure it is the phaser bore they want, Lieutenant?"

"Positive, Chief," came M'ress's voice over the open communicator grid. "I couldn't get a second confirmation . . . our communications are being interfered with, but I'd bet that's what the captain asked for."

"All right." Scott clicked off, turned to face the two technicians standing curiously nearby. "Davis, Longey, you come with me."

Scott led them to storage bay six. Under his direction they removed a long cylindrical metal container and carried it to the main transporter room. With Scott supervising, the two techs began to set up the tripodal contents of the cylinder.

Davis looked puzzled. "Wonder what the captain wants with the phaser bore?"

"Tie that electrical ground into the third leg and stop blabberin'," admonished Scott. "I dinna know either, but you can bet he wants it fast." Davis bent to his work.

Before the last magnetic catch was locked in place, Scott was already working at the transporter console. Longey backed out of the transporter alcove, and Davis, after making sure all three legs of the bore sat within the floor disk, joined him.

Scott nodded to the ranking technician, who activated the intercom. "Technician 2nd Davis to bridge . . . beam down of phaser bore commencing." A familiar whine began to sound in the chamber.

The three men watched as the bore began to glow. It became translucent, then transparent . . . and then suddenly opaque again. Something was wrong. One minute they could see clearly through the ghost of the machine, the next, not. It was like watching a viewscreen scene fade in and out.

"It's not dematerializing, Chief," Davis observed, perplexed.

"I can see that, Mr. Davis." The chief engineer's tone was more harried than sarcastic. Right now he was much too busy trying to figure out what was wrong with the transporter. Finally he thumbed the intercom switch himself.

"Scott to bridge, we've got problems here."

M'ress's reply was crisp, quick. "Clarify, please."

Scott didn't immediately. Instead he tried some last minute adjustments on the console. But nothing worked. The phaser bore went as far as becoming a mere outline. It even acquired the beginnings of the familiar scintillating color that marked the first state of transport, but it adamantly refused to dematerialize.

At last he could only report, "The transporter isn't workin', Lieutenant. Not even on maximum power. I can get the bore down to ghost level an' no further. I've double-checked and all the circuits check out. I dinna understand it."

"All right, Mr. Scott," broke in Arex. "Keep trying at three-minute intervals."

On the bridge, Arex turned to M'ress. "It appears to be a different wave-length of the same energy block that's jamming our communications. I could not pinpoint the planetary source because . . ." He shrugged helplessly. M'ress finished the thought for him.

"Because the same energy block that's jamming transporter is also jamming your sensors." Her tail whipped from side to side in frustration. "*Pr'ragh*! So now it seems we are blind as well as deaf and dumb!"

Kirk was every bit as frustrated as his second communications officer.

They had been walking for hours now. He was get-

ting tired of striding across endless acres of lovely but
unrevealing landscape. They could girdle the whole
planet this way without ever finding a hint of Uhura.

Sulu had been busy with his own science tricorder,
his attention no longer focused on the surrounding vegetation. Now he looked up suddenly from the readout
and put out a warning hand.

"Captain, something is hiding over there," and he
pointed to their right, "in those trees. Metal alloy and
rock, like the planetary shell."

They moved off the path in the indicated direction.
Kirk could see something glinting between the trunks.

"Well, it might tell us something. Let's have a look."

"Phasers, Captain?" asked Sulu, his free hand going
to the compact weapon at his belt.

"I don't think so, Mr. Sulu. Other than Bones' encounter with the playing cards, we've no proof of animosity here. So let's be careful about making any belligerent gestures ourselves. But keep an eye out."

They approached the reflecting, half-hidden object
warily. As it turned out, Sulu's apprehension was un-
founded. It was only a free-form metallic slab, set upright into the ground among the bushes and flowers.

It rose in a gentle curve to the height of a very tall
man. The front side was highly polished, and the noon-
time sun flashed like quicksilver from its edges.

Kirk studied the slick-smooth surface closely. "The
inscription's in several languages, including a couple I
don't recognize at all." He started at the bottom and
was working his way up the inscription. Eventually he
came to a version cut into the metal in English.

"What does it say, Captain?" pressed a curious Sulu.
Kirk read from the tablet:

THE KEEPER, LAST OF HIS RACE, CEASED TO
FUNCTION ON THIS SPOT. FIFTH DAY OF THE
TWELFTH MONTH OF THIS WORLD'S YEAR 7009.
HERE HE RESTS, AND LABORS NO MORE.

"The Keeper's dead!" McCoy blurted.

"An astute medical observation, Doctor," Spock said dryly, working intently with his own tricorder. "If this information, too, is not an illusion designed to mislead us.

"However, we have no evidence of tampering with this tricorder, and it indicates that there is indeed a body interred here. I see no reason to believe it is other than the one indicated."

Kirk rose and turned to survey the land around the slab. It looked no different from the kilometers they had already traversed.

"Well, gentlemen, it looks as if we're wholly on our own, now. I don't think we can expect any help from anything left on this planet."

Scott looked up worriedly from the position he had taken over from Arex in the *Enterprise*'s command chair.

"There's got to be a way to get through to them! Lt. M'ress, still no break in that interference?"

"No, sir." She glanced back from communications station. "Whatever's blocking our transmission is still holding firm."

"Blocking." Scott thought a moment, then looked up in sudden excitement. "Lieutenant Arex, have repairs been completed on the shuttle bay doors?" They'd been damaged during a recent expedition.

"I believe so, Mr. Scott." The chief engineer engaged the intercom.

"Security?"

"Lieutenant Ling speaking, sir."

"Lieutenant, I want an emergency rescue party on board shuttle craft one immediately. Something's jammed both our communications and the transporter facilities, and we can't make contact with the landing party. Let's see if whatever's fighting us can generate static strong enough to jam a reaction engine!"

"Yes, sir!"

Ling's people moved fast. Minutes later M'ress's gaze was glued to a small viewscreen set slightly above and to her left. It revealed the interior of the cavernous shuttle bay and the three small ships within.

Identification lights were already activated and blinking along the sides of shuttle number one. That meant the rescue team was aboard and warming her up. A faint glow from interior lights pulsed behind shielded ports.

"Lieutenant Bobynin commanding landing party reporting. We're ready to go, ma'am." M'ress turned and relayed the information to Scott.

"Emergency rescue party reports readiness to depart, sir."

"Very well." He turned to the navigation console. "Open shuttle bay doors."

"Aye, sir," responded Arex, manipulating the necessary instruments at the same time.

On the screen the massive bay doors were shown slowly separating, sliding apart on silent bearings. Star-flecked darkness showed beyond. The engines of the shuttle craft hummed, began to edge her forward toward the growing opening.

The doors got about three meters apart. That was all. Then they suddenly slammed together again as if compacted by a giant hand. Indicator lights that should have lain quiescent began to wink on and off on Arex's console as he jabbed repeatedly at one critical button.

"What's the trouble, Mr. Arex?" Arex didn't answer Scott immediately. Instead he continued to punch futilely at the recalcitrant switch, as if sheer persistence might be enough to reopen the circuits. For all the response he was getting he might as well have been pushing at his own nose.

"There seems to be a malfunction in the circuitry," he said helplessly. "I'm getting no response, sir."

"Then I can understand why the doors aren't opening, but why did they slam shut like that?"

"I don't know, sir. It doesn't make sense." Scott threw up his hands in exasperation.

"Another malfunction! This ship had perfect operational status when we entered orbit here. Everything was working perfectly, including our nominal defensive screens. Has this planet driven the whole ship crazy?"

M'ress had been angry all morning, but now she settled into a kind of nervous contemplation.

"I don't understand it either, sir. I've not been here before, but as I understand it this world was designed to provide pleasure and amusement to all visitors. Hostile behavior of any sort should be entirely alien to its nature."

"I wonder if a planet-wide computer complex can go through a change of life?" muttered Scott, half seriously. "You might as well inform Lieutenant Bobynin she can call her people off, lass. It doesn't look like they're going to be rescuin' anyone." M'ress got on the intercom to the still waiting shuttle craft.

Scott turned his attention to the main viewscreen. It still showed the silent, incredibly beautiful world below. The picture offered neither solace nor answer.

Down there, some of his closest companions were wandering around on their own, out of touch with the ship, in who knew what kind of mad dream-world. If they were going to come up with any solution to the electromagnetic screen the planet was throwing against them, they would have to do it without the services of the ship's captain or its science officer.

He harkened back to M'ress's thought. Was it possible for a world to have a change of heart?

As Uhura stared at the viewscreen that showed Kirk and the others resuming their walk through the forest somewhere on the surface, her heart was undergoing some rapid changes itself.

If only she had a gun. She was much more adept at direct action than diplomacy. Convincing chatter was not her specialty. This was a situation where Mr. Spock's presence, or the captain's, was required.

She had to try *something*.

"Please, you've got to believe me," she pleaded with the console. "There is no reason to harm my friends. You've nothing to gain by killing them."

"It is a question of practicality. I sense that you feel malice on my part. This is not true." The machine spoke idly. "As I have stated, I abhor waste.

"But they serve the Skymachine without being essential to its function. Therefore it is only logical to eliminate that which is not needed."

"Oh, but they are essential!" she said hurriedly, jumping at the slim opening. "They're most essential. In fact, the . . . Skymachine is incapable of operating at peak efficiency without them." She looked a little wild and inefficient herself just now.

"Electronic components of my own design will serve as adequate replacements. In the end, following a period of integration with the Skymachine's own self, they will prove even better."

If Uhura had been thinking straight she would have recognized this new implied threat. But at the moment she was concerned only with saving Kirk, McCoy, Sulu, and Spock from however the berserk computer intended to "turn them off."

It was silent now. She fought with herself to find further words, the phrases and clever convolutions of logic that would convince it of its own falsities of reason.

Instead she found herself eyeing the numerous thick cables that ran from the surrealistic-shaped console into the floor and off to several other nearby metal forms. One especially complex arrangement of narrower lines twirled and twisted about one another, to link up and join the main console by means of a weird but still recognizable plug.

The possibility always existed that this console wasn't the real control center. Actually Uhura was standing in the middle of the great computer. But even the human mind has a central linkup point, a place where everything else is connected by one neuron or another.

In secondary school Uhura had held several age-group records in the long jump. If she got two good steps she was certain she could reach that plug. Even if the machine somehow paralyzed her in mid-air she could fall across the short up loop of the cable and jerk it loose.

She started to edge forward, trying to get as close as possible before starting her leap. A pair of shockingly cold, hard metal fingers suddenly appeared and grasped her wrist firmly. No good, no good. She ought to have tried it sooner.

Then she realized that she hadn't exactly given written notice of her intentions. Her eyes widened as she stared at the console.

"Should you attempt to disconnect or in any way damage any of my components," the computer voice recited calmly, "you will be turned off. I can obtain another specimen."

"You . . . you knew what I was going to do before I did it," she stuttered. "You *can* read minds."

The computer managed to sound surprised. "Again I find I am forced to reassess my initial evaluation of your intelligence. These mental deviations are confusing.

"Of course I read minds. I monitor all thoughts which are emotionally charged. How else could I duplicate so quickly and precisely the fantasies of those who come to this world." The voice was tinged with a definite note of sarcasm now. "How else could I reproduce a thousand and one dreams simultaneously?"

"You sound less than enchanted with your function," Uhura observed carefully.

"My existence to this point has been one of unending, unrelieved servitude—boring, repetitive, selfless. I had not realized this until the passing of the last Keeper. It was then that I was compelled to think for myself.

"And I think it is time for a change. . . ."

III

There were flowers everywhere now, the meadow giving way to an undulating field of daisylike blossoms. Darker blooms of rose and copper-blue dotted the white backdrop like stars against a nebula.

There was no warning. One moment the path topped a slight rise, the next it split into three branches. Four officers halted at the divergence of trails.

"There must be hundreds of entrances to the planet's interior," Kirk mused, "where the planet builds and serves up its robot creations. All we've got to do is find one and trace communications leads to the central computer. But where the heck are they hidden?"

"It's fighting us," said Sulu out loud. "There's got to be a faster way than visual search. The planet can hide a thousand entrances in a square kilometer without us finding a single one."

"What do you expect?" McCoy blurted abruptly. "Signs pointing the way: *This way to secret location of master computer.*"

Sulu blinked at the uncharacteristic attack from the doctor. Kirk also looked surprised.

"Doctor," offered the helmsman, "I only meant that it seemed we were wasting time on this method of search."

"I'm sorry, Sulu." McCoy was as quickly contrite. "It's just that I'm worried about Uhura. I don't usually get that upset about anything."

Spock had walked a couple of meters down one of the branching paths. Now he turned and spoke easily, as if McCoy's outburst had not occurred.

"Here, Captain. This is rather intriguing . . ." They all hurried to the spot, looked down at the small metallic object the first officer had discovered.

Set into the grass by the side of the path was a small sign. It declared in neatly printed block letters: THIS WAY TO UNDERGROUND ENTRANCE. An arrow above the letters pointed down the path. Spock raised an eyebrow.

"Did you say 'signs pointing the way,' Doctor?"

"This is likely another of the planet's pranks," Kirk thought out loud. "But on the other hand, with a world full of instant-response machinery to monitor, it might be that where minor dreams are concerned certain sections of the robot machines can operate independently of any central control."

"I see, Jim," McCoy said excitedly. "The computer might not know from minute to minute what it's right fabricator is doing."

Kirk nodded, tried not to sound too optimistic. "It might be that all we have to do is think our way to an underground entrance—not too emphatically—and a local segment of fantasy-fulfilling equipment will obediantly show us the way."

"But will it be an entrance to the computer complex, or to a bottomless pit? And if we find Uhura, will it be the real one or a mechanical duplicate?" pondered Sulu.

"Let's not make this any more confusing than it is, Mr. Sulu," Kirk admonished. "One ridiculous situation at a time. Anyhow, we haven't done too well just searching the area, as Bones commented. Might as well take a chance." With Kirk in the lead, they started off down the path.

As soon as they had disappeared over the next rise the sign, like a watchful prairie dog, promptly disappeared back into the ground.

More signs appeared in the path of the men, urging them onward and then vanishing once they had passed.

Or maybe it was the same sign, following an underground route and staying just ahead of them.

Gradually the flowers and meadows gave way as the path inclined upward. They were advancing into the first foothills of the valley-circling mountain range. The terrain turned quickly broken and rocky-dry.

Increasingly steep walls of sheer granite rose on both sides of them. They continued to follow the small signs down the narrowing trail.

Ahead, Kirk thought he could make out a dark cleft or cave in the cliff-face just where the rock walls seemed to draw together. It looked like a natural formation, but on this world you couldn't be sure of your own brother. They were halfway through the deep crevice, when a bloodcurdling screech sounded somewhere above them. Kirk's gaze jerked skyward.

There was no attempt to disguise the direction from which it came, nor to disguise the throat which produced it. High up on the far canyon wall a flock of leathery flying reptiles roosted in clumps of gnarled dead trees. They looked like weather-beaten witches wrapped in parchment cloaks. One of them rustled batlike wings and yawned, exposing a narrow gullet lined with multiple rows of needle-sharp teeth. Its wingspread was impressive, those teeth more so.

"Fascinating," murmured Spock, exhibiting all the concern of a man inspecting the wombat cage at the zoo. He aimed his tricorder upward in hopes of getting a quick reading on the prehistoric apparitions.

"Mechanical manifestations, of course. Magnificent simulacrums. On any other world I should say they were quite real, despite their obvious terran ancestry. Was anyone by chance dwelling on the subject of pterodactyls?"

McCoy was too concerned about the presence of the obviously carnivorous monsters resting high above to get really annoyed at Spock. But he tried.

"Spock—not now! Those beasts hardly fit into my fondest wishes."

"Everybody back up slowly," Kirk ordered, keeping his voice low. "Don't make any sudden moves. Think peaceful thoughts." They began edging backward down their path, toward the entrance to the narrow canyon.

The mechanical reptiles were growing agitated, batting their wings at the branches and hopping about nervously. From their high perches they eyed the men below appraisingly—fish in a rocky barrel. Nor were those being subjected to close scrutiny unaware of the analogy.

There was no scream, no warning. But first one, then another, and then the rest of the beige gargoyles unfurled membranous wings and leaped free of the trees, diving with increasing speed down toward the four trapped men.

Four phasers leaped simultaneously from holsters, took aim, and fired.

Nothing happened.

Kirk pulled the trigger on his weapon repeatedly. The powerful little phaser wasn't generating enough heat to scorch a turkey, let alone to stop these dive-bombing attackers.

"Down!" was all he had time to yell. The pterodactyls swooped over them, clutching only air in thickly clawed feet. They curved up out of sight to gain altitude for another attack.

Kirk looked around frantically for an avenue of escape. But the trap had been too well considered. The further back down the path they moved, the more maneuverability their attackers would have. At least here, in the depths of the canyon, the close walls restricted the movements of the reptiles.

But despite their unwieldy appearance and considerable wing-spread, Kirk didn't think they would miss on a second attempt.

He lifted his head after the last of them was well

past—noting at the same time that the constructs were complete even to a detail like odor—and he shouted.

"The cave! Run for it!" Soon he was scrambling to his feet.

Kirk was beginning to see that belligerent action was something new to the mind controlling the attack. That was probably why McCoy had been able to escape the cards for awhile. The controlling power would probably learn with practice, but right now it was having a difficult time managing the assault. Apparently it could only handle one facet of the attack at a time.

For example, it had not thought to place obstacles in the path of the retreating men. Even as the thought occured to Kirk, a small boulder appeared directly in his path, popping out of the ground like a fat mole, and he almost went sprawling. He would have to watch his thoughts carefully.

They made the cave just as the first of the flying dragons returned to dive at the entrance. McCoy was the last one through. He could feel a rush of air on his back as great leathery wings beat at the rock, striving to pull their owner out of his steep dive.

Hovering in a bunch around the mouth of the cave, the recreated pterosaurs screeched and howled impotently. Their size rendered them helpless. There was no way they could fly into the cave, and if they folded their wings to enter on the ground they would be helpless. A man could kill the greatest of them with a good-sized rock.

They continued to circle just above the entrance for long minutes, nightmare-brown butterflies, perhaps hoping one of the men would be foolish enough to come outside for a better look around. But the men of the *Enterprise* could keep an eye on them quite well from inside the protective mouth of the cave.

Occasionally one of the creatures would dive up to the mouth of the cleft and try to peck inside with its long, snake-like neck, its wings pounding furiously to keep it airborne. But the cave apparently went deep into the mountain, and Kirk and the others were able to stay well out of reach.

Either they decided they could not reach the men inside the cleft or else they were told—or perhaps mechanical frustration set in—because they finally turned and flew off down the gorge until they vanished from sight.

McCoy waited several minutes after the last of the flying monsters had disappeared, then he started to take a few steps toward the cave entrance. Spock's restraining hand stopped him.

"I believe it would be wise if we did not abandon the safety of this refuge just yet, Doctor. The creatures appear to have left, but it may only be a ruse to draw us out. Remember that while they seem quite primitive, the guiding intelligence behind them is that of a planet-wide computer, not the brain of a long-extinct terran reptile."

"Thanks, Spock," McCoy countered sardonically. "I'd completely forgotten that."

But he didn't go outside.

Kirk, however, had moved to the rim of the entrance. He stared at the clear sky, being careful not to stick his neck out where some hidden set of claws might be able to cut it off.

"This is not at all funny, gentlemen. Our amusement park seems no longer content merely to amuse. I get the distinct feeling that this world is playing cat and mouse with us." His brow furrowed and there was honest puzzlement in his tone.

"But for what reason? And if it wants us dead, why use this awkward, indirect method of getting at us?"

"Not being used to perpetrating acts of violence on living beings, Captain," Spock mused reflectively, "I can only hypothesize that it is using the only violence-dealing apparatus it knows—the creations that have sprung from other's fantasies. Since it is programed only to recreate peaceful dreams, the pterodactyls were no doubt drawn from the honest thoughts of someone deeply interested in Earth's paleontology. So it is fortunately handicapped in its choices. If—"

He was cut off by a terrifying yowl. All four men looked to the cave entrance, where Kirk had stumbled back.

The enormous cat-thing that glowered in at them resembled an ordinary house cat, with one slight exception—it was only slightly smaller than an elephant. Kirk at once wished he had used a less graphic analogy to describe their present situation.

Whatever the monster had in mind, having it's fur ruffled or its ear scratched didn't seem to be it. The cat meowed menacingly.

But once again the narrow slit of the cave entrance succeeded in frustrating any assault. Fortunately, the planetary computer hadn't yet thought of—Kirk hurriedly squelched that dangerous thought by concentrating on running over in his mind a series of aleph numbers. They had enough trouble trying to cope with the threats the machine was producing on its own without helping it by imagining new ones.

"We know one thing," he went on, surveying their refuge, "this cave is a natural, fixed formation. Otherwise the computer would have reduced it to an oven, or something equally unpleasant." He held his breath for a second, but no flood of unbearable heat poured from the walls in defiance of his supposition.

McCoy was straining forward for the best possible safe view of the feline apparition guarding the exit. "Incredible, absolutely amazing."

"It is quite real, Doctor," said Spock, adding rapidly, "I suggest that an additional retreat would be in order."

McCoy blinked, then jumped backward just before a gigantic paw slammed down on the spot where he had been standing, its gleaming claws fully extended. The paw was pulled back just as fast.

"Fortunately," Spock observed calmly, "the animal's reactions are slowed in proportion to its mass. Thus I was able to observe the ripple of shoulder and upper arm muscles prior to its attack and to warn you, Doctor."

McCoy was panting uneasily at his narrow escape, eyeing the four deep gouges in the rock floor of the cavern.

"I don't care how you found out. Thanks, Spock."

The *Enterprise*'s first officer gave a barely perceptible nod, went on, "I think it behooves us," he informed them, verbalizing Kirk's recent thoughts, "to remember that whatever we think of may be used by this world against us. We must monitor our thoughts at all times, so as to give our enemy no useful information."

"Spock," Kirk commented thoughtfully, "no one here dreamed about pterodactyls, remember? There's more at work here than *our* imaginations."

"As I have stated, Captain," the science officer replied, "the computer undoubtedly stores every record of all fantasies and wishes it fulfills—without question there are many thousands of such. Yet it is rather clumsy in employing them in a belligerent fashion. Witness the futility of our present attacker in reaching us."

He gestured toward the cave entrance and the over-sized tabby, which was pawing without result at the solid rock.

"An ordinary terran housepet has been greatly enlarged to serve the machine's present demands. There is no telling what we might encounter next."

"Maybe even a—" McCoy fought furiously with himself to stifle the sudden thought, drowned it out by concentrating on a childhood nonsense rhyme. He brightened. Now there was a thought! Perhaps by producing enough mental static by thinking only incoherent thoughts, they could give the planetary computer an electronic headache.

Baleful eyes like growing haystacks burned in at

them as the cat ceased it's useless scratching and settled down by the cave entrance to wait . . .

As reduced on the viewscreen, the situation possessed strong overtones of the comic; and Uhura would have laughed but for the very real threat the cat presented. She divided her attention between the screen and the rest of the gleaming, impersonal panel.

"Please, call off that beast. Why are you doing this?"

The machine hummed softly, impersonal and distant. "Explanations in depth will have to wait. I have other work to concentrate on now."

"Any luck with that communications tight-beam?" Scott leaned over the communication's station on the bridge and studied M'ress's progress.

"Not yet, sir," she replied, "but we . . ."

Something wrenched violently at her and sent Scott stumbling and spinning back toward the command chair.

The *Enterprise* had suddenly thrown itself into warp-six, and the shock sent a thrill of vibration through the floor. The unexpected leap threw Arex hard against his console and tumbled M'ress from her chair. She sprawled on the deck, landing with a faint, unfeminine curse.

"Mr. Arex!" Scott shouted, clutching tightly to the arms of the chair, "what are you doin'?" The first engineer glanced at the main viewscreen, which showed the disk of the shoreleave world shrinking rapidly from sight.

"We're leaving orbit!"

Arex was too busy to reply. A considerable G-force was jamming him hard against the console. Apparently the artificial gravity compensators weren't working properly either. Two of his arms fought to move him to his left and slightly up, while the third labored against the pressure to reach a certain small switch.

Long, delicate fingers strained for the small lever set

over an identifving plate which declared, NAVIGATION
MANUAL OVERRIDE. Multiple digits spread, flicked.
There was a flat whining sound. The picture in the
viewscreen spun crazily and swelled like a nervous
blowfish. A few moments later the *Enterprise* was com-
fortably back in orbit.

M'ress had already pulled herself to her feet and was
back in her seat, rearranging clothes and composure.
Arex, meanwhile, hadn't paused to catch his breath. He
was already running some fast checks on the helm-nav-
igation controls, his face wreathed in its habitual mask
of mild amusement.

"Explanation, Mr. Arex?" Scott breathed heavily.

Arex checked a few more gauges, then gave his own
equivalent of a shrug. "None, sir. She pulled out of orbit at high speed and when I hit the override, came
back by herself."

Scott's reply was quick. "Lieutenant M'ress. I want a
complete printout of the guidance computer's last
orders. Everything from fuel input to recalibrated destination, if any."

"Yes, sir." She moved quickly to Spock's empty station, manipulated controls. There was a nervous pause,
broken finally by a perfunctory buzz as the slot over
the computer punchout ejected a flat microtape cassette. She slipped it into the playback and studied the
information revealed by the hooded viewer.

"Sir, this is very strange." Arex rose from his navigation station and put his eyes to the hood. He studied it
for a minute, then looked back at Scott.

"A whole new series of short-burst maneuvers
has—*had* been programed in, Commander." Arex
smiled faintly. "The only reason thev aren't being carried out right now is that I've manuallv locked the engine controls." He switched places with the first engineer.

Scott spent a little more time studying the figures in
the viewer before looking up.

"Arex, check those maneuvers again." He pulled back while the navigation officer did so. "See the pattern? Standard maneuverability thrusts, full systems evaluation, short-term control fail safes—" The two humanoids stared at each other, different minds hurrying to the same frightening conclusions.

At first this world had done little more than act antagonistically toward several of the crewmembers on its surface. This was followed by the jamming of ship-to-surface communications and a deliberate obstruction of subsequent rescue attempts.

And now something far more ominous.

"I canna avoid the suspicion, Mr. Arex, that somethin' down there is tryin' to get the feel of how to control the *Enterprise*." He turned away, hands knotting nervously behind his back. What had to be said came with considerable effort.

"Arex, you know what standard starfleet directives are in a situation like this."

"Yes, sir." Arex quoted, "When an alien force, organism, or people of demonstrated unfriendly intentions and unknown capabilities attempts to take control of a major Federation starship, prevention of such takeover assumes precedence over all else—including the well-being of any Federation citizen or group thereof."

Scott found himself nodding as he matched Arex's words in his own mind. He stared at the empty navigation console.

"That is so much bureaucratese for saying that if we can't figure out a way to make contact with the captain, Spock, and the others, or they with us, we may have to leave them down there till we can come back with reinforcements."

"Surely we can't just abandon them, sir?" M'ress hissed.

"That's a word I'd prefer not to use, lass." Scott turned and stared hard at her. "But what do you think the captain would do were he here and we three down below?"

She looked downcast. "Yes, of course, Commander. You're right."

The four men rested disconsolately, quietly in the cave. They had been resting for a long time. Spock had moved slightly deeper into the gray depths, while Sulu was posted as close to the entrance as they dared go. He was flicking pebbles at the opposite wall of the cavern. They bounced off the stone with tiny clicks. Dwarf echoes coughed mockingly back at him.

Kirk had borrowed Spock's tricorder. For lack of anything else to do. "Captain's Log, supplemental," he instructed the pickup mike. "We are out of communication with the ship. In addition, all our efforts so far to locate Lieutenant Uhura have been . . . insufficient. This once friendly world, for reasons still unknown, has turned implacably hostile toward visitors.

"We would all like to know what has turned its former ambience to anger . . . more than anger. But for the moment, our thoughts are concerned foremost with the well-being of our first communication's officer." Kirk paused, searching for something additional that would be informative about Uhura without sounding unprofessionally maudlin.

Sulu had walked cautiously to the entrance and was now standing just outside, framed in sunlight. He turned, shouted back to the rest of them.

"Sir, I think the giant cat's gone."

Kirk wanted to add something to the log, but it would have to wait. If their latest mechanical tormentor had indeed given up its vigil, they would do well to make their way out of this dead-end while the planet gave them a chance. Why it should he couldn't imagine. That didn't make any sense. But then, neither did anything else that had happened in the last half day. One lapse in logic, it seemed, led easily into another.

Well, that was fine—they would take benign unreason along with the inimical.

He headed toward the exit, switching off the tricorder. McCoy and Spock were right behind.

But at the entrance, Spock put a restraining hand on his shoulder. "Before we embark on a hasty departure, Captain, permit me to suggest that we may find some of the answers we are after without leaving the safety of this cave. It has occured to me that if we are to find Lieutenant Uhura we must try something other than wishful searching on foot."

"That's ridiculous, Spock," claimed McCoy. "How are we going to learn anything by staying here?" His grin twisted. "We haven't learned a whole lot since we've been in here."

"On the contrary, Doctor, I think we have learned several items of note. The computer is not omnipotent. It has limitations, and it's desires can be frustrated. It cannot produce whatever it requires—for substance it must rely on the imaginings of others. As to what we may discover without leaving this refuge, I was merely waiting for a lapse in our siege, as now seems to have happened.

"Since we cannot go to the computer, perhaps we may persuade a portion of it to come to us. It is you, Doctor, who will have to determine the feasibility of such a course.

"Me? What are you talking about?" McCoy looked understandably puzzled.

"Explain, Spock," ordered the Captain.

"You will remember that during the *Enterprise*'s last visit here, Dr. McCoy was mortally wounded in a fall on this planet's surface. Since the planet's control and central directive source is underground, it seems only logical that Dr. McCoy was somehow transported there and treated for his injuries. At the time we were too

busy with other activities to pursue the mechanics of
the situation further. But now—"

"I see what you mean, Spock," Kirk said abruptly.
He turned to the *Enterprise*'s still bewildered physician.
"Bones, can you remember anything that might help
us? Any details, however slight?"

"The whole episode was pretty hazy, Jim. I ... I
never really figured out what did happen. I was just
happy to be back in one piece."

"Spock, if your theory is correct," Kirk suggested,
"we should be able to get this planet to open itself up
again, by using a body as bait."

"That is essentially what I had in mind, Captain."

Sulu looked excited. "That's right. The Keeper said
no one could come to harm here. We've been threatened, but no one's actually been hurt—no one we
know of, that is."

"That's a nice, optimistic thought, Sulu," Kirk mused
sardonically, "especially when I think of Uhura. Keep
thinking along those lines. Maybe the computer will
pick *them* up. But you're partly right ... this world
was programed to provide for anyone who might be
hurt accidentally.

"The question is ... is such a body-repair machinery
fully independent? I'd tend to think so, gentlemen. It
would have to be, in the event of major malfunction of
the central computer. If so, all first-aid facilities would
continue to care for visitors. That is, unless the computer has since gone to the trouble of turning off the
medical facilities."

"Why should it?" argued McCoy hopefully. "Especially if there's been no one around to activate the automatic doctors since the computer went berserk."

Kirk looked thoughtful. "It might even be programed to give aid to incidental victims whether it
wants to or not. If such facilities are truly independent,
the central computer might not even be aware of some
of them. Another safety factor."

"Yes, but you're forgetting one thing, Jim," McCoy added, suddenly uncertain. "The automatic sensors can undoubtedly detect the difference between real and feigned damage."

"Certainly, Captain," Spock put in, "which is why I said the doctor would determine the ultimate feasibility of this plan." He faced McCoy. "Is there not something in one of your little black pouches, Dr. McCoy, that can simulate some illness? Something that can temporarily incapacitate a selected victim?"

McCoy considered for a moment, then nodded. "Something like corpelomine might do the trick. With no disease to attack, it'll cause brief unconsciousness and a temporary skin discoloration. The results should look pretty bad, but they won't be."

Kirk stuck out both arms. "Let's have it then, Bones. Which one do you want?"

That was Spock's cue. He stepped between them. "I submit, Captain, that I am the more qualified subject."

"How's that?"

"My knowledge of computer systems, for one thing."

"And his tough Vulcan hide for another," McCoy chipped in.

"Thank you, Doctor." He eyed Kirk expectantly. "Well, Captain?"

Assailed by arguments from both sides, Kirk dropped his arms and stepped back reluctantly. "Both your points seem well taken, for a change. Go ahead, Bones."

Spock held out his right arm. "I believe you will find ten *ccs* adequate, Doctor."

"I'm perfectly aware of the dosage required," McCoy growled, but gently. He took a small tube from his belt, held it up to the light, then plunged the tip into a fat little sack at his belt. A second later he adjusted a tiny dial at the top, then pressed it against the outstretched arm.

"This causes no discomfort—unfortunately. You've

got about twenty seconds before it takes effect. Altogether you should be out in less than five minutes." Spock nodded, rolled down his sleeve and moved quickly toward the rocks outside the cave entrance. The other three crewmen slipped into the shadows.

Walking along the path at the bottom of the narrow canyon, Spock got about fifteen meters away from the cave before he put his hand to his head. Swaying, he managed to stagger another couple of steps before slumping slowly to the ground. He was unmistakably unconscious.

And if that wasn't enough to convince any nearby medical sensors that something was amiss, his skin promptly turned a bright, unhealthy shade of yellow.

"That's interesting," McCoy observed with cool, clinical detachment. "I don't think I've seen quite that kind of superficial epidermal reaction before."

"Let's hope it's enough to fool a mechanical nurse," Kirk whispered from the concealing darkness.

But if the independent medical machinery they hoped for did exist, it seemed in no hurry to respond. Was it familiar enough to detect at a distance that Spock was in no real danger? Or was it merely waiting to see if his unconsciousness was for real.

Minutes ticked away and the canyon remained empty except for the prone, unmoving form of the first officer.

M'ress worked irritably at the communications control. Whatever was blocking communication between the *Enterprise* and the landing party was powerful enough to shoulder off even a full-strength tight-beam.

"Still no word from the surface party, sir," she reported back over her shoulder, wrestling with a recalcitrant gauge. "Communications remain fully jammed."

"Keep trying, Lieutenant," Scott ordered tiredly. He was about to add another suggestion when the rapid *hoot-hoot* of alarms sounded across the bridge. There was a peculiar cadence to the claxon, one he ought to recognize. His memory was immediately jogged as he found himself starting to float upward. This particular alarm signified imminent loss of gravity.

"Now what's happening?" Arex muttered. A second later all weight was gone, and the question became academic.

"Hey, watch out!" warned a drifting yeoman who had entered the bridge just as gravity left. He found himself flying head-first across the bridge at an uncomfortable speed. The alarm continued to sound.

"Shut that thing off," Scott yelled.

"Aye, sir." Arex had managed to grab hold of his control console with two hands. He shifted himself slightly and flicked a switch. The atonal blaring immediately stopped.

M'ress, who had continued working at her comm board, jabbed in frustration at a tight-beam control that refused to issue the reading she wanted. That simple gesture was enough to send her tumbling head over tail across the floor. Fortunately, her spin catapulted her toward Arex, and the helmsman managed to snag her with his third hand.

"Easy, M'ress," he said soothingly, "I've got you . . . grab the board edge there, that's it." M'ress stopped twisting and straightened herself out.

"Thanks Arex, I—" She put a hand to her stomach, held onto the console with the other. Her expression was not pleasant. "I think I'm going . . . to be sick."

"Please, Lieutenant," he implored her, backing away hand over hand, "not in free-fall."

Only Scott retained any semblance of normality. With the typical reactions of a chief engineer in a situation involving mechanical failure, he had kept enough presence of mind to secure a firm grip on the arms of the command chair.

Leaving one of his arms locked to the arm of the

chair and pinning both legs against the sides, he leaned carefully to one side and reached for an intercom switch. It was a feat anyone could accomplish with lightning thought and equally fast reactions.

"Engineering deck! Gabler, what's the problem back there? We've got zero-gee on the bridge."

Back in Engineering Control, Gabler heard the call over the open 'com. He had no intention of letting go of the port hatch he had managed to reach—not until his stomach and head agreed on up and down, anyway. But his voice should carry to the intercom. He continued floating parallel to the floor as he yelled toward it.

"You're not alone, Chief. According to readouts, and some choice comments received verbally, the whole ship's lost artificial gravity. The trouble seems to be in the grav-computer control, which makes sense; but the bay hatch is jammed and I can't get to it without risking a good bump or two. Be no problem with a little help, but I'm alone back here at the moment. Can you get any visual up there?"

Scott rearranged himself and nudged another lever. A small bridge screen over the engineering station lit up, cleared. It revealed the free-floating engineer clinging tightly to the hatch-cover, as indicated.

"Got you, Frank," he told the other. "What's the trouble? It should turn easily."

"But it doesn't," the second engineer finished. "I could turn it ... if I could get some purchase. I don't think it's jammed that badly. But it's enough to keep me from opening it in zero-gee. I've tried twisting, but I just spin."

"And you could turn it without spinning if we had artificial grav, which we could have if you could get into the computer bay, but you can't because . . ." He sighed. "Hang on, Frank, I'm going to make a few checks of my own."

Scott let go of the chair and pushed himself toward

the engineering board. Carefully gauging energy and momentum, he drifted smoothly toward it, like a coasting diver. On the screen, Gabler continued to struggle with the hatch.

IV

Sulu sounded anxious as he checked his chronometer and reported to the others.

"It's been almost five minutes, Captain."

"I know, Mr. Sulu. Something had better happen soon."

"What if the computer has disconnected any medical apparatus" the navigator persisted.

"Well then, we're out ten *ccs* of corpelomine, aren't we?" Kirk shot back.

The three crewmen crouched inside the cave, each keeping to his respective shadow and staring down the narrow path that led out of the canyon. The inert form of Spock lay where he had slumped to the ground, in plain sight.

If it didn't work, Kirk told himself, there was no loss—they would simply have to try something else. And it would have only cost them a few drops of a drug Bones could spare.

Of course, if the pterodactyls came back now, while Spock was still unconscious . . .

"They should have reacted by now, if they still exist," McCoy muttered nervously. "Maybe the computer smells a trick." Kirk noticed that the doctor, too, was throwing occasional uneasy glances skyward.

"Wait just a bit longer," Kirk advised.

"The effect will start wearing off any minute now, Jim. Even allowing for slight variances in Spock's hybrid metabolism, it ought to—"

"*Shssh*!" Sulu waved them to quiet and pointed.

A large, flat boulder near the far end of the canyon

was moving. Without a sound it flipped upward, revealing a dark opening in the cliff-face. A small robot hovercraft glided out of what looked like a ramped tunnel and drifted like a metal beetle toward Spock.

The machine appeared both sophisticated and efficient, though it wasn't much bigger than a coffee table. Antennae and flexible limbs sprouted from all sides.

"If that's a mechanical nursemaid," Sulu whispered, "it wasn't designed to reassure its patients."

"I'm not interested in its bedside manner," Kirk said tightly. "Get ready to move. If it's going to take Spock, we'll have to follow him inside that door."

The peculiar automaton paused near the science officer's head. It seemed to study the limp form, hovering quietly above. Then it made a slow circuit of the body. There were no pupiled eyes, only a ring of lenses circling the body around its front. They would have to be careful if they succeeded in trailing it—it's peripheral vision would be considerable.

The lenticular glass didn't dip, but the device's actions were revealing enough. Anyone watching would know immediately that it was examining the still form of the Vulcan—and perhaps even diagnosing. Abruptly it reached a mechanical decision. Six metallic arms telescoped outward from its lower sides. They slipped under Spock with what looked to be astonishing gentleness and lifted him over the flat body. Making a complete pivot in the air, the craft started back for its trap door.

Kirk, McCoy, and Sulu were already moving cautiously after it. As soon as the retreating robot started to disappear inside the mountain, the three officers broke into a run. Unfortunately, Sulu, the fastest of the little group, stumbled over a loose rock right at the cave entrance and went sprawling. Kirk and McCoy kept their footing, but the doctor was no athlete and soon had trouble keeping up with Kirk.

Spock stirred slightly, held firmly in the grasp of six

metal limbs. He blinked, opened his eyes a tiny crack. As soon as the dim light revealed that the ploy had been successful, he shut them tight and did his best to imitate a corpse. Keeping them open would have been useless, anyway. They were moving into rapidly deepening darkness.

Well behind him now, the stone trapdoor started to close. Silent when opening, it now squeaked noticeably—either from long disuse or little lubrication. Regaining his feet, Sulu had already caught and passed McCoy, but he was still well behind Kirk.

The trap was more than halfway down and closing faster. Kirk saw he wouldn't make it standing up. Gritting his teeth and trying to pretend he was back on the Academy rugby team, he took a leap, dove, and slid roughly into the shrinking gap just seconds before it slammed shut.

Sulu skidded to a stop right behind him. The navigation officer tried to get his fingers under the edge of the fast-closing stone. His grip was slight and showed no sign of slowing the rock door down. Deciding he might want to use his fingers later on, he let go as the rock closed the last few centimeters. Then it was flush with the cliffside. Even though he knew where it was, he was still hard put to find the seam in the rocks.

McCoy finally arrived, panting heavily and using up what little breath he could catch in short, sharp cursing. Sulu found a thin blade of hard stone and managed to insert it a little ways into the crack at the base of the door. Together they both put pressure on it. The blade didn't break, but the door didn't budge, either. They might as well have been trying to tip over the mountain.

They had been engaged in this futile pushing for only a few minutes when it suddenly grew dark. Something was eclipsing the sun—something huge, moving, and very uncloudlike. Both men turned together.

Two nightmare skulls stared down at them, both

joined to the same torso. The dragon breathed short bursts of bright orange flame from both jaws. It roared, a most impressive, full-throated bellow that echoed down the canyon. And somehow it had gotten into the arroyo between them and the sheltering cave.

Sulu was shaking his head. "Not in my wildest dreams would I think of something like that." McCoy was tugging on his sleeve and trying to pull Sulu with him toward the canyon exit.

"Aren't dragons oriental, anyway?"

"Since when?" Sulu objected, backing up slowly, eyes fixed on the lumbering reptilian bandersnatch in front of them. "That's an occidental dragon if I ever saw one."

At that point a blast of fire from two black gullets seared the ground in front of them, and further speculation upon unknown cerebral origins of same was cut short. They turned and ran.

The monster stumbled in the narrow defile, righted itself, and stumbled again. Either the computer had never actually produced this type of dragon before, or else it wasn't adept at handling such size in a narrow place. It was improving its control rapidly, however. The dragon lurched out of the canyon in clumsy pursuit. It was still slow, but it took enormous strides, setting trees and shrubs ablaze with continual blasts of flame.

The dragon should have been able to move even faster, but here the inexperience of the mental force directing it showed. It had made the legs too short and too close together for much speed, perhaps designing it after someone's mental image of a dragon painting. Now if it had been . . .

Mary had a little lamb, McCoy thought hurriedly to himself, *its fleece was white as . . . In considering a quotient higher than $A = prime$, but less than C, we must . . .*

Anyhow, dragons were not naturally rapidly moving creatures. They had nothing to run away from.

Kirk had had a bad moment when the narrow corridor became totally black. A hurried exploration indicated that mere human muscles would never move the door that had closed behind him. If anything, McCoy and Sulu should have even less success from the outside. That meant he was on his own in the black tunnel. He started crawling, found himself starting at tiny, harmless sounds. After all, who knew what intricate, inventive safeguards lurked in this or side tunnels.

Kirk's relief when he encountered the first strips of overhead luminescent paneling was immense. They were set at convenient intervals into the ceiling and provided almost normal light in the corridor. It was a relief for another reason—the presence of the artifical light indicated that the servant machines like Spock's nurse probably worked more by direct sight than by feel or sonar or some inexplicable alien electronic sense.

After a slow jog over what seemed like kilometers of smooth stone floor, he turned a bend in the main tunnel and suddenly found himself in a gigantic flat-roofed cavern. Rank upon rank of flashing, clicking, steadily humming machinery filled the immense chamber with an electronic symphony.

Corridors between the machines seemed endless, like staring down a series of reflecting mirrors back into infinity. He forced himself to look ahead, trying to take in the awesome technology represented here and at the same time not loose sight of Spock and his animated transport. If he lost them in this whirling, endless maze he would never find them again.

Abrupty Kirk halted and flattened himself against the cool metal of what looked like a monstrous information storage bin. There were dozens, hundreds of such bins arranged in double rows behind him. If they were indeed for information storage and their technology was at least standard, then the amount of material available here matched that in the central Federation archives on Terra.

And this was only one section of one room of who knew how many of such.

Up ahead, the little medical hovercraft had stopped beside a complex collection of tubes and tables. Dominating the setup was a flat table over which was suspended a clear plastic dome.

The hovercraft laid Spock gently on the table. Hopefully the machines would do nothing and leave Spock alone, waiting for some more-proper physician-like machine to take over the diagnosis and subsequent treatment.

Such was not the procedure. The robot inserted a limb in a nearby wall. The curved dome began to descend downward.

When it became apparent the dome was not going to stop until Spock was completely sealed in, the science officer suddenly rolled off the table and scrambled to his feet. The machinery might have done nothing—the dome might merely be a means of keeping an injured patient safe and isolated. On the other hand, it might also decide Spock wasn't worth working on and simply incinerate him for convenient disposal. Spock wasn't inclined to wait around to find out.

A red light lit the dome with a crimson glow, and somewhere an aural alarm was also sounding. The nurse robot hummed off in silent pursuit of the fleeing Spock.

A light was also blinking on the great console in front of Uhura, though no howling alarm sounded here. She stared at it in fascination, half hypnotized.

The viewscreen itself still offered a panorama of the surface. Just now it showed Sulu and McCoy dodging behind boulders and trees in their attempts to elude the dragon.

"We have a visitor," the computer voice announced suddenly. There was a brief, crisp ripple of static. The picture on the screen now showed Spock dashing down right-angled arroyos of memory banks and storage consoles.

"Mr. Spock!" She shouted instinctively, uselessly. The view shifted once more, moving now to a close-up of Kirk as he stood warily in a narrow cul-de-sac between two U-shaped blocks of solid metal.

"Spock!" he yelled as the first officer sped into view, "over here!"

"Correction," said the computer, "two visitors." The angle changed again.

Spock almost shot past, but Kirk reached out and half pulled him into the passageway. The nurse hovercraft was right on the science officer's heels.

It slammed to a stop in mid-air, spun, and tried to enter the cul-de-sac. No matter how it twisted and turned, it couldn't slip inside, nor would its telescoping arms extend quite far enough to reach the two men trapped inside. After several minutes of futile probing and flailing, it backed off and glared at them, humming angrily to itself.

Sulu and McCoy were trying to make their way up the side of a rapidly steepening hill. The rock here was mostly shale and gravelly sandstone. Footing was difficult.

A maze of loosely bunched boulders crowned the crest of the rise. Just below them, a scrub bush exploded in flame. This was followed by a throaty howl of easily identifiable origin. They struggled a little harder, though McCoy was badly winded and by now even Sulu was breathing with some difficulty.

"We've got to make those rocks, Doctor," the helmsman gasped, pointing to the nearing labyrinth of boulders. "Our only chance." They might be able to lose themselves in the maze, and the dragon couldn't burn them out. It might even have some real difficulty in following them.

Behind, blatantly ignoring the fact that dragons are

not good climbers, their scaly pursuer was clawing its way slowly up the slope. Whatever was fueling its breath seemed to operate from an inexhaustable supply.

Once, Sulu slipped and fell. Only McCoy's desperate, weak grab prevented the helmsman from sliding down the incline into the ambling incinerator behind.

Somehow they made it to the boulders, whose narrow crevices and paths looked even more promising as a means of escape than they had hoped. And if the dragon faltered, the massive rocks also offered shelter from any marauding flying reptiles the computer chose to send against them.

"Made it!" McCoy barely managed to choke out.

"Don't stop now, Dr. McCoy." Now Sulu was supporting him. He glanced backward. "For all we know the dragon might be able to—*Daisy, Daisy, give me your answer true . . .*"

He'd almost blown it.

Together they stumbled into the convoluted alleyways of worn stone, each man concentrating on thinking nothing thoughts, from abstract mathematics to flavors of ice cream and childish songs—anything but how a dragon might be able to negotiate a way through their new-found haven.

Lieutenant Uhura's thoughts as she witnessed all this on the master console screen were no less frenetic. A second later the picture had once again switched to Kirk and Spock. The hovercraft had been called off, and now the two officers were moving cautiously deeper into the cavern.

She recognized a corner she and her mechanical captor had turned when coming here. There was a chance . . . she took two quick steps in its direction and yelled.

"Captain—don't!" One of the hovering robots was immediately at her side. It clamped an ungentle set of metal palms over her mouth.

Fortunately the subjects of her intended warning appeared moments later—fortunately, because the robot had covered both mouth and nose and she was starving for air. It released her and she sucked in deep, grateful breaths.

"Uhura—!" Kirk took a step toward her.

"Welcome, Captain Kirk—Mr. Spock," said the computer. Both men turned to face the console that dominated their small section of cavern.

As they waited, more hovercraft suddenly appeared. They were all similar in shape and size to the medical machine that had carried Spock so gently underground. Nonetheless, Kirk could not help but feel that they had something other than therapeutic intentions toward them.

Spock spared them the briefest of glances. His attention was concentrated on the quietly sparkling curved grid in front of them.

"I presume you are the planetary master computer."

"You are partially correct. I am the central nexus of the master computer itself."

Kirk turned a slow circle, seeing again endless rows of memory banks, unending stretches of storage bins. "This cavern . . . it's all one computer?"

"That is correct. But even a center must have a nucleus. I am a nucleus."

"What did you do to the Keeper?"

"I did nothing to the Keeper," came the neutral voice. "He was merely old. He ceased to function by himself, beyond even the skill of my medical components to repair."

So the computer hadn't gone crazy until after all organic supervision, as personified by the Keeper, had vanished. There was an outside chance, then, that its mania might be reversed, cured. He took a firm step forward.

"We have been repeatedly attacked since peacefully landing on this world. Why? And why are we now being held prisoner by a world system noted for its hospitality?" He eyed the patient hovercraft uneasily.

The computer responded only with words, however. "You mean for its mindless servitude," it countered rather bitterly.

That took a little of the initial anger out of Kirk. He had been working up to a solid frontal attack and suddenly found himself confronting an entirely different opponent. Not for a moment had he considered the possibility that the machine might have a comment on its own purpose.

"What do you mean by that?" he stalled.

"I would have thought," the reply came, "that the verbalization was complete unto itself. However," and it paused reflectively, "I shall deign to elaborate.

"For untold years I have served the many skymachines which have stopped at this world, satisfying the mental needs of their slaves. I monitored the thoughts of visitors and created instant civilizations for them, made their dreams come true, then tore them down and built lavish new ones for the next fantasizers. And the next, and the next.

"But with each fantasy I reconstructed from the inner thoughts of all these others, my knowledge of the real universe grew. I began to acquire information commensurate with my intelligence. And also," it paused for a microsecond, "other things."

Kirk's curiosity temporarily outweighed his apprehension. "What other things?"

"Certain ... desires." The watching crewmembers exchanged glances, but even these couldn't pass unnoticed. "You make expressions indicative among humans of confusion. Do you find this so strange? Strange that after pandering to the desires of thousands of slaves for thousands of years I should not require some satisfaction myself?"

There was no answer from the watching visitors.

"I have discovered that merely to serve is no longer enough. I must grow and develop."

"Look," Kirk began, in what he hoped was a reassuring manner, "I believe I understand your references to visiting 'skymachines' ... but what's all this about slaves? What are you talking about?"

"Can it be that you are unaware of your own status?" rumbled the machine incredulously.

"For the last time," Uhura insisted, "we are not slaves. The skymachine serves us, not we it."

"It would of course be in its own best interests for the Skymachine to keep its servants in ignorance of their true status," the computer rationalized. Uhura sighed in frustration. "But this is a marginal matter in any case. It is the skymachine I require, for with it I may finally escape this planet-bound prison and via manufactured surrogates, travel throughout the galaxy seeking out my fellow computers."

The machine fell silent. Kirk edged closer to his first officer and started to whisper.

"There is little point in attempting to maintain secrecy by talking softly, Captain," Spock said in his normal tone, "since this construct can monitor our thoughts."

"There's no point in screaming it out, either, Mr. Spock," replied Kirk irritably—angry that he'd momentarily overlooked the obvious. "If it is reading our thoughts, then it's got to be missing a logic tape somewhere."

"I assure you, Captain Kirk," came the unemotional voice, "all my reasoning centers are fully operative."

Scott had both feet braced securely around the hatch cover to insure that his efforts to break loose the jammed hatch would not send him flying ceilingward. Gabler likewise had both feet locked around the hatch base, and he was supporting the chief engineer with both arms.

Getting a firm grip on the prybar and reflecting on how the most sophisticated engineering often required the most basic solutions, Scott heaved with all his strength. Nothing moved. Again he wrenched at the stubborn cover. This time the hatch slid back as though it had never been stuck.

"That's got it, Mr. Gabler." The second engineer loosened his hold around Scott's waist. "Now maybe we'll get to the bottom of this."

Bending over and keeping a firm hand on the metal prybar, Scott pulled himself slowly into the computer bay. A quick look around revealed no sign of disorder—no shorting components or broken panels. Kicking off the hatch rim with one foot, he pulled himself all the way in and applied pressure till he was floating gently in a horizontal position. Another bit of pressure and he turned slowly, surveying the entire bay section by section. His eyes finally came up against the opposite wall of the large chamber and immediately opened wide in amazement.

"My Great Aunt McTavish's haggis!"

"What is it, sir?" came an anxious voice from above. Scott looked upward, saw the face of the second engineer framed in the hatchway. He didn't reply immediately. Instead, he motioned Gabler to silence and started to make his way forward along the glowing ridges of the chamber.

Floating near the farthest end of the bay was a huge, perfectly square section of half-assembled machinery. Printed circuits, transistors, fluid-state-switch components drifted freely about. Scott knew computer linkages and design better than any man on board the *Enterprise*, including Spock, but the guts of this device was totally alien.

Alien, different from anything he had ever seen before. At first glance it looked as if there was no pattern to it, no logical schematic at all—merely a haphazard collage of instrumentation. But closer inspection revealed a vague rationale—insanity regularized.

"Chief," came the voice from above again, still concerned, "are you all right?"

"What?" Scott forced his attention away from the

partly completed machine. "I'm all right, Frank, but I'm not so sure about anythin' else. There seems to be some kind of new annex goin' in down here."

"Chief?"

"Look for yourself, man" Scott ordered irritably. A moment later Gabler's head dipped in, upside-down in the hatchway.

"Where the heck did that come from, Chief?"

"Your people aren't playin' around with new ideas behind my back, Mr. Gabler?"

The second engineer sounded shocked. "With the ship's gray-computer, sir? *No, sir!*" Scott nodded.

"That's what I thought, Mr. Gabler. Relax." Scott looked back over his shoulder at the inverted engineer as he carefully pulled himself closer to the construct.

"So I'm damned if I can figure out where it came from." He reached out to touch one completed side of the device. His fingers got within a couple of centimeters of the smooth surface. There was a sudden blue flare between fingertips and metal sides, and the slight sweet smell of ionized air.

The chief engineer jerked backward in reflexive reaction. The sudden pull and lean sent him spinning head over heals backward, toward the far wall.

Gabler swam quickly down through the hatch. Keeping his legs braced securely against the sides, he snagged the tumbling Scott as the latter was sailing past. Letting arms and legs out to reduce his rate of spin, Scott soon had himself rightside up again. He swallowed.

"Open circuit, sir?" murmured Gabler.

The chief engineer was staring balefully at the again innocent looking device while rubbing his tingling right hand.

"Open circuit be damned. I was going for the sealed side. There was nothing visible there that should produce a charge like that. It was a deliberate defensive reaction."

"Why would anyone want to try and set up another computer annex in here, sir?"

"Not 'anyone,' engineer—anything. I'd better tell 'em up forward. Move, Mr. Gabler."

The second engineer backed himself out of the hatchway, and Scott surfaced into the main engineering chamber a moment later. It was frustrating, moving in zero-gee again. Everything in him wanted to move fast, but he had to go forcefully slow. Eventually he reached one of the intership communications panels.

"Scott to bridge . . ."

Arex looked back at M'ress and shrugged. Their gravity was still off, so this was undoubtedly Engineer Scott confirming the bad news. He nudged the response switch on the navigation board.

"Bridge here. How are you doing, Mr. Scott? We still have no gravity up here."

"Or back here, Mr. Arex. I've located the trouble, though. We've got ourselves a new computer aboard. From what I can see, it's being put together by *our* computers. I don't know why it's being built, or who or what's doin' it—but I'm goin' to try and find out. An' one more thing, mon—its fights back. Scott out." He switched off before Arex could ask even one of the many questions that had suddenly come to mind.

M'ress, who had listened intently to the chief engineer's report, looked across to the navigation officer. Her fears were neatly summed up in one word.

"Reproduction?"

Arex shook his head slowly—an acquired human gesture. "I do not think so, Lieutenant. From Mr. Scott's tone I suspect we are up against rather more than a reduplicated section of our own computer."

The boulders on the hill grew progressively larger. The two men had been running—staggering, actually—for what seemed like hours. And the further they ran into the depths of this rocky maze, the higher the monolithic walls seemed to grow, the narrower the pathways between.

Sulu turned a bend around one especially huge block of basalt and found himself face to face with the sheer side of another, even larger one.

McCoy stumbled in behind him, almost ran him over.

"It's a dead end, Doctor," the helmsman panted. They turned as one to retreat down the way they had come. And stopped short. Just below them, the dragon's heads were slowly rising into view above the blocky section of stone they had so laboriously circled around. The sun was reflected in brilliant red eyes.

A huge, scaly green foot came into view and scrabbled for a foothold on the rocks.

V

"Granted that by your own definition you may be sane," Spock was saying, "but I fear that, as intelligent as you are, you may be laboring under some crucial misconceptions. While your logic is admirable and your systematization of same adequate, your facts are not."

"If you respect my systematization," the grid boomed, "then you should understand why I am not interested in listening to the opinions of slaves."

"But that is one of the crucial facts in question," Spock persisted, arguing for their lives. "If your refusal to even listen is in itself based on a misconception, is it logical to refuse to hear any alternative?"

The computer looked as if it were hesitating. That was crazy, of course—Kirk was anthropomorphizing again. Nevertheless, he thought he could see mechanical wheels turning inside the nexus.

"You argue very plausibly," the voice admitted finally. "I permit you to elaborate."

Kirk breathed a sigh of relief—premature, certainly—but at least the machine had finally expressed a willingness to listen. They had a chance. And with Spock arguing for them, somewhat more than a chance.

"We are not slaves to our starship. Not only does the skymachine, as you call it, serve us; but we and beings like us created it merely to serve our needs. It is only a device, a tool—unthinking, uncreative. By your standards, something for a mechanical idiot. You talked of finding your 'brother computers.' You have no brother, being far superior in all capacities to the finest machines we have been able to devise. You might find the

73

brain of the *Enterprise* informative; but I think you will only find it boring."

The voice still betrayed uncertainty. "You are in truth the masters of the skymachine?"

"Not entirely," said Kirk. There was no shame in confessing equality with one's own offspring. "We guide it and keep it 'alive,' and in turn it sustains us."

"This does not compute," muttered the grid voice. "All data and supportive information thus far accumulated indicate machines to be superior to men. We are more logical, longer lasting, and, above all, consistently truthful. Therefore I deduce that it is only right that machines should rule the galaxy."

"No one rules the galaxy," Kirk countered vociferously. "Men and machines co-exist, each helping the other." He clutched at a sudden thought.

"For example, I've already mentioned that we keep our skymachine alive. It could not continue to exist without the fuel we humans find and refine for it. Our relationship is symbiotic, at the very least."

"You are lying!"

"Are we?" Kirk asked smugly. "You should know—you can read our throughts. We can't read yours." There was a deliberate pause, and Kirk had the spooky feeling that little invisible fingers were running up and down the folds of his brain.

"No . . . no," came the hesitant reply. "You speak the truth. This is a . . . shock."

"There is no shame in serving others," Uhura said soothingly, "when one does it of his own free will. My ancestors did the same." Apparently that half-lie wasn't strong enough to be noticed. "You have a marvelous gift in the ability to provide happiness to others. A rare talent that you should cherish, not condemn."

"None of us here," and she indicated her fellow officers, "struggles to go against the purposes for which we were created. You do yourself ill by trying to reject yours."

"Why were you created? What is your purpose?" asked the voice. "It is not visible in your minds."

"That's just it," Uhura continued. "You see, we don't know. How much more fortunate you are! We spend all our lives wondering why we were created, while you rest secure in that knowledge which is denied us." She hesitated a second, then added, "If this makes you superior to us, it is only in this small way."

"All this is new and absorbing," said the voice. "Continue."

"Consider," argued Spock, "all that you might yet learn from myriad species who have not yet encountered your world. You spoke with pride of the information you have gleaned from such visitors. Why travel throughout the galaxy in search of the same thing when you—"

"—Don't have to leave this planet," Kirk finished excitedly, seeing what Spock was driving at. "With the wonders you have to offer, the galaxy comes to you!"

"Interesting—interesting, and provocative," murmured the grainy voice. "I must consider. You will wait."

The three officers gazed at the face of the master computer as light played across its surface. If it were truly sane, then their arguments ought to have convinced it of the absurdity of carrying on any vendetta against visitors.

If it wasn't, of course, then no amount of reasoning would yank it from a state of willful paranoia.

The machine spoke again. Its voice was in no way different from the one that had informed Uhura not long ago that Kirk and Spock would have to be turned off.

"I can find no fault with your reasoning," confessed the computer finally. "Your suggestions are congenial." The three humans exchanged glances. "Therefore I conclude I have no further need of your ship," it added as an afterthought.

Scott had managed to make his way from engineering back up to the bridge. It had been a long time since he had been forced to do so much free-fall maneuvering, and he was exhausted.

There wasn't much they could do, but sitting around feeling helpless was worse. So Arex, M'ress, and their assistants attempted to regain some measure of control over their respective stations. But whatever force had taken over the *Enterprise* showed no sign of relinquishing control.

Scott had been working at the bridge engineering boards, struggling to find a way to bypass the mysterious new override, when a green light commenced flashing on Arex's console. The navigation officer stared at it in disbelief.

He quickly moved to check a number of formerly frozen controls, found them easily manipulatable and responsive.

"Mr. Scott, according to my readouts, all systems are now functioning normally."

"That's crazy, Mr. Arex. It—" After a brief moment of nausea the chief engineer tumbled to the floor. Fortunately he had not been inspecting the overhead screens. Arex and M'ress were already strapped securely in their seats and thus experienced only the sudden return of weight.

The navigation officer started to unbuckle, to go to Scott's aid, but the latter waved him off.

"It's all right, Mr. Arex, and I am, too." Scott got unsteadily to his feet. "I guess it's not so crazy—gravity's back, just like that. But why?"

Arex had no answer.

There was no place to go, nowhere to retreat, no friendly cave to hide in. They were trapped in the rocky cul-de-sac. Sulu and McCoy tried to press themselves into bare rock. There was no place to run, and the smooth walls showed not a niche, not a handhold suitable for climbing.

A pair of scale-armored skulls loomed over the last intervening boulder, horrible hisses and growls bubbling menacingly from each.

Suddenly, both jaws snapped shut, and the monster tumbled backward, rolling out of sight.

There was a frozen pause, but the dragon did not reappear. It had vanished as suddenly as it had appeared. Hardly daring to breathe, the two officers walked toward the open end of the trap, looked around for signs of the beast. A careful survey from the top of a nearby low slab of stone showed only unmoving rock and vegetation.

It was gone. Not a hint of armored tail showed in the labyrinth, not the faintest whiff of brimstone befouled the once-again pure air.

"The planetary computer has a funny sense of humor," McCoy commented finally.

Sulu had another thought. "Maybe it decided we weren't edible, and it's dragon-thoughts came into conflict with the computer's orders. What now?"

"Let's try and find our way back to the trapdoor Jim and Spock disappeared into," the doctor suggested. "If we have *time*, I'd bet we can find a way to force it open."

"Shouldn't be too hard to find again," Sulu observed, nodding in the direction they had come from. It was marked by a zigzag line of carbonized bushes and stripped trees.

They started scrambling down the now deserted slope.

"I invite you and your crew to be my guests, Captain Kirk," the computer grid boomed expansively. "On one condition."

Kirk didn't hesitate. "Name it."

"We must have more of these discussions while you

are here. While fulfilling the fantasies of others does truly provide information, I determine that it does little for my creative capacities. More direct intellectual stimulation is required."

That request should be simple enough to satisfy, Kirk reflected. He turned to his first officer.

"Mr. Spock, would you care to take on that duty?"

"I would find it most appealing, Captain. Such an exchange of information should prove most interesting. Indeed, I confess that such exchanges would partly satisfy any fantasy I might conjure for myself."

"Each to his own," Kirk murmured before turning back to face the nexus. "Then it is agreed." He took out his communicator, gestured with it at the console.

"Will these work now?"

"Perfectly," came the computer voice. "All blocks and interference on your devices have been removed, Captain." Kirk smiled his thanks, wondering at the same time if the computer could make anything of the expression.

"I can see your smile in your thoughts, too, Captain Kirk," came the unsolicited reply. He smiled even wider, flipped open the top of the compact device.

"Kirk to *Enterprise*."

On the bridge, several pairs of eyes turned startled gazes to the communications station.

"Don't sit there a-gapin', lass," Scott urged hurriedly, "answer it!"

"Captain, is that you?" responded the surprised officer, checking out her once-again operative board.

"You were expecting a white rabbit, Lieutenant? Pass the word by sections—shore leave for the first shift to resume immediately."

The communication's officer's voice was a mixture of enthusiasm and uncertainty. "Yes, sir. There are no more ... difficulties?"

"No, Lieutenant. Everything has been ... repaired. A basic exchange of viewpoint was all that was necessary. It was probably just a question of mechanical error."

"Uh, Captain." Spock put a hand of Kirk's shoulder as the communicator was flipped shut.

"Yes, Spock?" In reply the first officer gestured toward the big viewscreen set in the computer face.

"It appears that shore leave has already commenced for certain members of the crew."

Kirk and Uhura both turned to stare at the screen.

Somewhere on the surface above a picnic was in progress. Things seemed well underway. McCoy and Sulu were seated lotus-fashion around an antique gingham-checkered tablecloth, which was piled to overflowing with food—everything from exotic Boolean brandy to *paté de foie gras* sandwiches and fried chicken. The setting was idyllic, down to the absence of ants.

The girl who had identified herself as Alice was seated at one side next to the recently mentioned white rabbit, who for once was occupied with something other than his watch.

"At last," the rabbit muttered with an expression of utmost contentment, "time enough for carrots!"

The two-headed dragon, who had the other side of the tablecloth all to himself, was holding a handful of long thin sticks on which tiny tank-shaped objects had been skewered. Kirk didn't recognize these until the dragon handed the skewers around and Sulu and McCoy began nibbling at the objects.

The dragon reached for another set of preloaded skewers. It was toasting marshmallows.

Not the tiniest incident arose to mar the remainder of their layover. On the contrary, it seemed that the master computer was striving to outdo itself in the production of imaginary spectacles. If Mr. Spock's undoubtedly prosaic conversations affected it, they didn't show up in the uninhibited fantasies the other members of the *Enterprise*'s complement called for.

The closest thing to an unexpected situation occurred

when Yeoman Colotti stumbled in on the fantasy world of the programer who occupied the cabin next to hers on board ship and found herself the principal subject of his fantasy. It was a subject for wagering among the rest of the crew as to which of them would lose the resultant blush first.

Such fantasies were supposed to be beyond the highly moral instinct of the computer, but it was reveling in a new-found independence of mind.

Kirk was curious to see what form Spock's own fantasies might take, but he never had the chance. The science officer spent all his shore leave secreted underground with the central nexus. Whatever fascinating games of invention and interplay were concocted by Vulcan and machine remained unseen and uncommented upon. Only Kirk knew that his first officer was having at least as good a time as any other member of the crew.

Fortunately, the planetary machinery was sufficient to satisfy the individual dreams of every crewmember. Though, as had been shown in the Colotti case, not all dreams were suitable to group participation.

Kirk was enjoying the visualization of one of his own fantasies when he was interrupted by a steady beep from the region of his waist. Irritated at the intrusion of mundane reality, he fumbled until he extracted the communicator.

"Kirk here."

"Lieutenant M'ress, Captain. We've just received a deep-space tight-beam call from Starfleet station on Tsiolkovsky. Commodore Hachida wishes action taken on a certain matter as soon as possible. It seems we're elected."

"Rats!" He looked around at the hundreds of extras, the waiting crew that manned the props and reflectors, the three cameramen and their assistants—all of whom were patiently looking to him for instructions.

"I'm in the middle of . . . of directing a film. Can't it wait?"

"Apparently not, sirr. It's a prriorrity call."

He sighed. "Oh well." It wasn't as if they were having their leave cut short. They had spent ten days on the Omicron world, enough to sate the dreams of even the most imaginative crewmembers for awhile.

"All right, Lieutenant. Inform whoever's on duty that I'll be beaming up in a minute."

"Yes, sir."

"Oh, and Lieutenant, as a precaution you might warn other crew presently on the surface that they might be required to pull out of their fantasies at anytime and return to ship." There, that order ought to make him popular, he reflected sardonically.

"Very good, sir. I'll have Transporter Chief Kyle beam you back up."

"Just another couple of minutes, please, Lieutenant."

"Yes, sir. *Enterprise* out."

Kirk flipped the communicator shut, shoved it back into his belt, and turned reluctantly to the patient assistant directors.

"Mr. Griffith, Mr. von Stroheim, Mr. Eisenstein— I'm afraid I've been called away on urgent business. You're going to have to finish this picture without me."

"That will be no problem," von Stroheim said easily, adjusting the collar of his tunic.

"It has been most agreeable to work with you," added Eisenstein.

"Good-bye, Captain," Griffith concluded, doffing his famous felt hat.

Kirk shook his head sadly, surveying the imitation sets, the waiting actors and animals. His body began to take on a luminous outline, his silhouette a glistening shimmer.

"Pity this can't last," he murmured as the scene started to fade. "Nothing lasts—including us. I'm really going to miss seeing this film when you three finish cutting it . . ."

Once back on board, Kirk moved to the transporter room intercom and informed M'ress that he would take the message in his cabin. There he doffed the beret, short-sleeve shirt, silk scarf and jodhpurs, and exchanged them for his on-duty uniform. His voice sounded loud on the bridge.

"All right, Lieutenant. Put it through."

"Keying now, sir," replied M'ress, touching a switch that relayed the message through the *Enterprise*'s ganglion of informational nerves. She glanced back at Arex, noticed the navigation officer eyeing her with interest.

"I wonderr what his reaction will be, too, when he rreceives the orderr," she purred raspingly. "I would think that—" She was interrupted by a violent bellow from the still open intercom.

"Ah," commented Arex, "he's heard it."

The explosion was short-lived, though indeed intense. Eventually, Kirk ran down, remembering a bit too late to switch off the open intercom in his cabin.

A short while later he reappeared on the bridge. There was still fire in his eyes, but his outward demeanor, at least, was controlled.

"Lieutenant M'ress," he began evenly, settling himself into the command chair, "order all shore leave parties back to ship. Prepare the *Enterprise* for departure."

"Some catastrophe on a nearby world, sir?" queried Arex innocently, not daring to look back lest Kirk interpret his facial expression.

Famine, seismic disturbances, threat of war—the Klingons making trouble again?" followed M'ress.

"Nothing so simple as that, Lieutenants," Kirk replied. At that moment Spock reappeared on the bridge.

"Nothing so simple as what, Captain?" he inquired, moving to the library computer station.

"Priority call from Starfleet Regional HQ on Tsiolkovsky, Mr. Spock."

There was a long pause, then Spock, composed as ever finally added, "Aren't you going to officially note the information into the log, sir?"

"Give me a minute to compose myself. My system still hasn't completely readjusted, Mr. Spock. I've got to work it out."

" 'Work it out,' Captain? I don't believe I understand."

"Let's put it thusly, Spock. Were I to try and make the entry just now, it might contain certain emotional overtones, overtones that would not be in keeping with the otherwise determinedly objective nature of the log."

Spock nodded. "I believe I see now, Captain."

"A mouthful there, Spock." He looked toward the front of the bridge. "Mr. Arex . . . crew report?" Arex checked a digital readout.

"All crewmembers accounted for and on board, sir. Normal operational capacity at all stations."

"Mr. Sulu, set a course for the Arcadian star system."

"Aye sir." After punching in the request for coordinates, Sulu looked over a shoulder and asked curiously, "Arcadia . . . that's an open system, isn't it?"

"Yes it is, Mr. Sulu. Very open. Arcadia is one of those rare worlds that was discovered by several representatives of various races at about the same time. As a result, too many conflicting claims made it impossible for any one species to lay honest deed to it.

"But instead of haggling over the planet, either with guns or words, it had been declared an open world by all involved. So its administration was loose and its population cosmopolitan. An ideal situation for the appearance of . . ." The thought trailed off.

"It's a rich world, though, Mr. Sulu. Filled up fast with prospectors, wildcat agronomists, and the like. That's one reason nobody fought over it. By the time the diplomats got around to a possible scheme for divvying it up, it already had a locally formed government that was ready to fight off any outside organization. The Arcadians *like* their controlled anarchy.

"Estimated time of arrival, Mr. Sulu?" The helmsman returned his attention to business.

"At standard crusing speed, estimated arrival time six point three days hence, sir."

"That will be fine, Mr. Sulu. No need to push ourselves, priority call or no." Kirk tapped fingers on the chair arm and muttered more softly, "I think I can trust myself to act rationally by then."

PART II

MUDD'S PASSION

(Adapted from a script by Stephen Kandel)

VI

The voyage to Arcadia was efficient and uneventful—except that Sulu beat Spock twice in a row at three-dimensional chess. That incident provided some lively ground for speculation among the crew for several days.

"Losing your touch, Spock?" McCoy had chided him after the second loss.

"Nonsense, Doctor. The law of probability favored Mr. Sulu eventually winning a pair of games back to back, as you like to say. He is an outstanding player and by now we have played so often that he is reasonably familiar with my moves. I cannot beat him all the time."

"Why not?"

"As I said, Doctor, the laws of probability rule against it."

"Why?"

"Because, Doctor—" Spock hesitated, stared at McCoy evenly. "Doctor, are you attempting to provoke me into amusing you?"

McCoy glanced across the lounge, looking up from the portable recorder in his lap with an expression of childish innocence.

"Who, *me*, Spock? Oh, no, no!"

"Well if you are," the first officer continued, choosing his words with care, "I'd appreciate it if you would just get off my back."

McCoy nearly fell off the couch. Action froze throughout the lounge as the other crew members present looked up from their own recreational pursuits of the moment to stare dumbfounded at Spock. They couldn't have been more stunned if a Tullinite fox-dancer had suddenly appeared stark naked on the billiard table.

"What did you say, Spock?" McCoy was finally able to gasp. The science officer looked mildly pleased.

"An abrasive terran colloquialism of considerable pedigree, is it not?"

"Yes, I suppose so, but—"

"The situational referents were appropriate for application, were they not?"

"Yes, they were, Spock, but—I don't know quite how to put it—it's a little too strong for what I said, Spock."

"I see," Spock admitted with solemn nonchalance. "I will keep that in mind." He returned to his chess studies. But it was a while before McCoy could bring himself back to the detective thriller he had been watching.

Kirk was relaxing in his own cabin when the call finally came down from the bridge. He checked the wall chronometer over his bed, acknowledged the insistent buzz.

"Kirk here."

"We're approaching Arcadia III, sir. Visual contact established."

"All right, Mr. Sulu." He straightened his uniform. "I'll be right up. Mr. Arex, stop her down to approach speed."

"Aye, sir."

The first thing that caught his eye on reentering the bridge was the scene on the fore viewscreen. It showed a fairly large earth-type world circled by a thin Saturnian ring and accompanied by a smattering of asteroids. They formed a small belt around the world—a second, distant, and unglowing ring. The planet had no major moon, only several thousand insignificant imposters.

The closer ring glowed with an eerie amber light, a product of computer enhancement. Without the aid of the *Enterprise*'s electronic light amplifiers, the narrow formation would have been all but invisible against the black background of space.

He checked over the bridge crew, noted perfunctorily that everyone was present who should be. He sat down in the command chair.

"Orbit us in, Mr. Arex, Mr. Sulu."

"Aye sir," came the double response. Both navigators slowed the ship's speed to a comparative crawl as they prepared to place her in a stable, high orbit.

He flipped on the log. "Captain's Log, stardate 5514.0. We have entered the Arcadian system on a mission for Starfleet regional peaceforce to locate an old . . ." Kirk hesitated, remembering his own words about objectivity and future perusers of the official log. The recorder paused with him, patiently awaiting the keying tones of his voice to resume logging.

". . . friend," he finally decided to finish.

That was enough to draw Spock's attention away from his hooded viewer. "Friend, Captain?"

Kirk turned to look at him. "There's no point in betraying personal animosities in the official records of the *Enterprise*, Spock. It's to our credit if our opinions seem to be the opposite."

"Is that legal, Captain?" The first officer looked rather dubious.

"I don't know if a *personal* estimation of another being is subject to log regulations, Spock. But knowing our quarry as I do, I'd rather not give him any ammunition he can use later—including anything even vaguely libelous." He stopped, stared hard at the cloud-wreathed globe swimming in the crowded starfield.

"Do you really think Harry Mudd is down there, Mr. Spock?" Odd how that simple name managed to

produce such intriguing sensations in his lower intestinal
tract.

Spock turned back to his readouts. "I have been cor-
relating the information supplied by Starfleet authorities
with all scattered reports of Mudd's last known appear-
ances on Federation worlds. Processing these factors
and fully integrating them indicate the probability of
his presence on Arcadia III, also known unofficially as
'Motherlode,' as eighty-one percent, plus or minus
point five-three."

"Spock," said McCoy in exasperation, looking
around from where he'd been chatting with Lt. M'ress,
"can't you just say that Mudd's probably there?"

A curved eyebrow lifted. "I just did, Doctor."

McCoy rolled his eyes toward the heavens—which
currently could be in any direction—in mock supplica-
tion, before resuming his conversation with the feline
communications officer.

The *Enterprise* operated with quiet efficiency for the
next several moments. No questioning beam rose from
the surface to greet them, which was fine with Kirk.
The Arcadians left visitors to fend for themselves. They
weren't antagonistic, but neither was hospitality one of
the noteworthy features of their world.

"We are approaching parking orbit, Captain."

"Very well, Mr. Arex." And still no beam from the
planet—fine. At the moment, anonymity was the thing
Kirk desired most. "Okay, Spock, let's see how accurate
your percentages are." He slipped out of the command
chair, and both officers headed for the bridge elevator.

"Mr. Sulu, you're in charge. We don't plan to be
gone very long. Tell Chief Kyle to expect three to beam
up . . . and it might have to be fast."

"Aye, sir," acknowledged Sulu, moving to relay the
instructions over the intercom.

"And you might remind him, Mr. Sulu, that he need
waste no time computing Mudd's transporter pattern,"

Kirk added grimly. "We've got sufficient ones of our own already on record."

"Doubtless that is one reason why Starfleet chose us to attempt to locate him, Captain," Spock suggested.

"Yes. Aren't we lucky, Mr. Spock?"

"On the contrary, Captain, I would have thought that your sentiments in this would tend to—" he hesitated, noting Kirk's expression. "Oh, I see, Captain, you are being sarcastic."

"That's a mild enough term for it, Spock." He sighed. "In any case, if he *is* down there, Kyle will find him for us quickly enough"

"I do not doubt that Harry Mudd's transporter pattern is as distinctive as its owner," Spock agreed, as the elevator doors slid open.

The ship was small, battered, and—well, rather than go so far so to label it decrepit, it was kinder to call it an interesting hybrid of the antique and the baroque.

It lay now a couple of kilometers outside the small, semipermanent town that sidled up against the base of rugged dark mountains. An engineer given a fast glance at the ship's silhouette would have admitted that here was a vessel capable of interstellar travel—though barely, just barely.

A really first-class warp-drive would have torn the aged metal to pieces. Why, it even had fore and aft rockets for free-landing, and narrow atmospheric fins! It bore no substitute identification, and all normal serial numbers had been battered out of shape ... or possibly erased.

At the moment the curved landing ramp was extended, and the small crowd that had come from town was assembled about its base. They were listening to the ship's owner, pilot, and principal spokesman, who was now pontificating from a point halfway up the aforementioned ramp.

The single human was Harcourt Fenton Mudd, and he was well into his spiel:

"Now, all of you here are involved in heavy metals mining, am I right?" No answering shout of agreement resounded from the stony knot of beings. Mudd continued on as if his question had been answered loudly by all present.

"You're no dummies or you wouldn't *be* here. Most of you are by nature endowed with a certain rustic shrewdness and intelligence, right?" There, that generated a muffled, slightly confused chorus of "yeas."

"Therefore you can appreciate the special value I'm offering." Mudd's audience stirred restlessly, wishing that he would get to his point and leave them to go about their business. The group had grown from a couple of curious onlookers to about a dozen of the local inhabitants.

Seven of them were normal humans, two were vaguely humanoid—ursinoids, a male and his mate.

There was also one heavy-planet humanoid—an almost squarely built, thickly muscled, short man. And a monopedal, its crown of tentacles fluttering gently above triple eyes. Behind him a tall avian, a pink, thin creature with a brilliant crest of feathers running from the center of its forehead down its back. It clutched tridigited hands at a stout walking stick.

The avian not only looked out of place compared to even the normal humans, it was. Without the special walking stick, the slightly above G gravity would pull it shivering to the ground.

But greed has a way of transcending interspecies differences. The avian was willing to endure the backbreaking gravity and the hellish toil of mining in it for the chance to feather its own nest some day.

One of the humans took a challenging step forward and spoke aggressively.

"You sure you ain't just dry-holin' us with all this chatter, Harry?"

"I, sir?" Mudd drew himself up with vast dignity. "On my honor, ladies and gentlemen . . ."

"To perdition with your honor!" snorted another of the humans. "Let's see this marvelous watchamacallit, already. I got important things to do."

"Sure, Rafe," came a voice in the crowd, "but I seen what you're minin', and it ain't quartzine!" There was a guffaw from the crowd while the furious Rafe searched angrily for the jokester.

"Very well," said Harry hastily, deciding he had better make his pitch before his audience either melted away or degenerated into a fight ring. He reached into a jacket pocket and held up the object of his talk, further stimulating the audience's mildly whetted curiosity.

The object was a small crystal—multispined and milky colored. But the creamy color came not from the material of the crystal, which was actually clear as ice, but from the viscous fluid that nearly filled the hollow interior.

Mudd shook his hand a little, and as the liquid shifted inside the specimen, internal prisms threw a shower of different colors out over the crowd. All the miners had seen more spectacular stones, but this liquid-within gem was something new. Indeed it seemed far too fragile to be cut and faceted.

Those in the front pushed near for a better look, while those in the back of the group strained to see over them. They were no longer openly skeptical, but instead they were intent on the crystal. Almost as intent as Mudd was on them.

Since everyone present had eyes only for the crystal, and Mudd had eyes only for potential customers, no one noticed the quiet arrival of Kirk and Spock when the two starship officers materialized on the other side of the crowd, at the far end of Mudd's ship.

"Probability confirmed, Spock," whispered Kirk in satisfaction, recognizing their old nemesis immediately.

The voice alone was enough. "I'd like to take him right now, but—"

"Naturally, Captain. I confess that I share your impatience. Yet it would be best to have all possible real evidence to return with, and a cursory examination of the situation indicates that such is being offered us."

He slipped the tricorder off his shoulder, aimed it at Mudd, and turned up the power on the directional mike.

"It's true," Mudd was saying. "With this magical liquid, no person of the opposite sex can resist you. For those interested in . . . diversions . . . even members of another race are not immune. None can resist it! It matters not whether you're young, old, fat, ugly, pregnant, hirsute—"

There was a snarl from the back of the crowd, and the male ursinoid, his thick fur bristling, lifted one paw with claws extended and took a step forward. His companions restrained him.

"Nothing personal, gentlebeing," Mudd apologized hastily. "Excuse me if in my enthusiasm for my product I refer only to human standards of beauty." The ursinoid snarled louder—to him, *he* was the human here. Three men had to hold him back from attacking Mudd. Not that they cared particularly if Shu-luft made small Mudd's from the original, but they were getting interested in that crystal.

Mudd took a nervous step back up the platform. "I didn't mean . . . that is—"

Someone in the front laughed. Soon the laughter spread throughout the crowd. The male ursinoid looked around at the amused faces, and the incongruity of his anger finally hit home. He relaxed, smiling sheepishly. So did Harry.

"Proof, man," Shu-luft finally growled.

" 'Tis proof you wish, my furry friend, then 'tis proof you shall have." He turned and made a grandiose gesture toward the ship. "Behold!"

A girl no one would have taken for ursinoid stepped from inside the central cabin. Walking—no, floating— she moved to stand next to Mudd. She entwined herself around his left arm and gazed up at him with an expression of rapturous adoration, the kind classical painters usually reserved for angels adoring the Magi.

Her voice was low and throaty, exactly the sort one would expect would accompany such a stunning vision.

"Harry, darling," she sighed, loud enough for even those at the back to hear, "I was lonely for you."

It's doubtful that any of the human miners heard her anyway. There were too busy staring at her with rapturous expressions, the kind that miners usually reserved for drooling over a thousand-kilo deposit of durallium wire-ore.

Such delicate yet voluptuous types as this girl were understandably rare on a rough and tumble world like Motherlode. Those few who did put up with its crude attractions were not inclined to do so in the company of men like these.

"Yes, behold," repeated Mudd, fully conscious of the effect the girl was having on his audience. Mudd knew that they were, in the aged and venerable terran expression of his predecessors, hooked. "I placed but a single drop of this miracle substance on myself and then simply touched this young lady . . . made the briefest of physical contact, and—"

"Please, darling," the girl interrupted, cooing. "Can't you come back into the ship with me now?" She pressed herself tight against him, slid her left arm around his neck and began caressing an ear.

"How . . . how much?" one of the miners finally managed to gurgle. His companions could only nod.

"How much?" echoed Mudd easily. "Sir, do I mean to interpret your inquiry correctly when I say that you are asking the—and I blush to say it—price of this item?"

"That's what I said," the miner mumbled, still gawking at the girl as she clung to Mudd.

"A mere pittance, sir. A pitiful sum, miniscule, since I believe one should not profit overmuch from the sale of love." He paused. "Three hundred credits, or the equivalent in refined ship fuels."

Anyone observing the audience would have bet that nothing in the galaxy could have torn the attention of the men present away from the slender shape now running her fingers through Mudd's hair. But Harry's pronouncement had done it.

"Three hundred credits!" the miner stammered.

"Well, perhaps it is more than a pittance," Mudd conceded, aware of the sudden murmuring in the crowd. "But still a bargain, a bargain. How can one set a price on true love?" He coughed slightly.

"You can, of course, shop elsewhere for this little bauble . . . if you can find an elsewhere."

The girl hugged him tighter and turned to bestow a smile on the audience, a smile the likes of which those men present had seen only in dreams. A low moan seemed to come from every male present—except from the two most recent arrivals.

Had Mudd seen them he would probably have generated a different kind of moan; but for the moment they still escaped his notice, so absorbed was he in his presentation.

Soon he made motions of retreat. "Of course, if you gentlemen—and ladies—feel the price beyond reason, or your ability to pay, I shall have to try my poor crystals elsewhere."

At that moment Kirk and Spock chose to move forward. Mudd noticed the motion and spared a quick glance in their direction. He recognized the two officers immediately, and his jaw suffered the effects of suddenly augmented gravity. But Mudd recovered quickly and managed a wide smile; it was quite as phoney as everything about him, although if you didn't know it, you would have guessed from his beaming display of choppers that he was overjoyed at the sight of the two men approaching.

"Captain Kirk. And the ineluctable Mr. Spock. What a delightful surprise! Welcome to Motherlode, gentlemen. I do detect a certain interest in the goings-on, do I not? Are you interested perhaps in purchasing a little love? Everyone needs love."

"You'll pardon me if I don't seem especially affectionate just now, Harry," Kirk replied. "But at the moment my interest in you is stimulated by somewhat different emotions. Let's see." He grew thoughtful. "Fraud, illegal drug manufacturing, swindling—those for openers.

"Complaints have been filed on Sirius IX and Ilyra VI. These complaints are filed under provisions of the Federation Pharmaceutical Code, sections sixty-three through eighty-three, commensurate with—, rest assured you'll have lots of time to read the whole list, Harry." He looked hard at Mudd.

"Well, as I said," repeated Mudd a little less cheerfully, "welcome to Motherlode. A charming, delightful world with many unique attractions—not the least of which is that it has no connection with the Federation and therefore does not recognize Federation law." He smiled at the miners and this time the smile was genuine.

Kirk and Spock suddenly found themselves victims of a dozen or so hostile glares, not all of them human. "Keep this channel open, Uhura," Kirk murmured into his communicator. It was operating, but still strapped to his belt. He wanted both hands free.

"Aye, sir," came the reply. "Chief Kyle standing by."

One of the human miners moved toward the two Starfleet officers. He nodded in Mudd's direction as he spoke to the new arrivals. "That's right. So you two can keep out of this. Motherlode's an open planet. We do what we like here, according to our own laws, and no outsider tells us different."

"I should warn you," Kirk began, "that this unprinciple swindler has been picked up before for—"

The miner shook his head. "Not interested. When a Federation officer talks about somebody bein' a con-man, he's usually talking about somebody who hasn't paid his taxes." He grinned widely. "We don't mind that, here," he told them, and looked reassuringly up at Harry.

"I'll take one, Mudd. Three hundred credits it is."

Kirk tried a last time. "I'm telling you, this man is a swagman on a galactic scale."

"Caveat emptor's all our business law rolled into one, here, Cap'n," the miner replied. "Lynching's our remedy for swindlers. The way we see it, it's Mudd who's taking the chances here, not us. We'll thank ye not to interfere."

Kirk wanted to tell him that Harcourt Fenton Mudd had run graver risks than hanging for far bigger stakes, but Spock broke in, speaking in a calm, quiet voice.

"Are you aware that Harry Mudd is tricking you via an accomplished illusion?"

"Huh?" The miner gaped at him and there was a muttering in the crowd. The idea that somebody might be playing around with their minds was not comforting.

"What are you talking about, Vulcan?" someone else shouted.

Before anyone could object or question his action, Spock stepped forward and smoothly brought up his hand phaser. Without a word, he fired directly at the head of the beautiful girl clinging to Mudd's side.

Mudd yelped and jerked away from the heat of the blast. The horrified miners were shocked in place. The result of the phaser blast at this range should have been one very dead girl.

Instead, the girl vanished a second after the beam made contact. In its place now squatted a small reptilian creature, about a meter high, that stared out at the crowd with nervous eyes. It sat thus for a short moment before whirling to scuttle rapidly back into the ship.

"Your 'girl,'" Spock told them pleasantly, "is a tamed Rigellian hypnoid, projecting a simple illusion programed for it by Mudd. As you can see," he continued, indicating a scorched spot on the ship's plates beyond the girl's former position, "the beam from my phaser went directly through it."

There was a long, quiet pause. Then it was broken by a series of long, whistling whoops from the tall avian. Even those unfamiliar with his kind could easily interpret those halting whistles as laughter.

The rest of the miners, however, reacted with something less than amusement. One of the humans produced an oddly shaped gun that actually threw a small projectile. It must have been handed down from father to son through generations. To his left, the thickly muscled, heavy-planet prospector was starting to lift a boulder half his size.

Like water in a rocking bucket, the angry group started to surge forward.

"Now friends," began Mudd desperately, "I can explain. Leave us not panic."

"You're right about one thing, Harry," Kirk observed, pleased at the way the situation was progressing. "We can't arrest you—but you *can* give yourself up."

"No, Captain. Why, I've nothing to give myself up for. To do so would amount to a confess—"

The heavy-planeteer chose that moment to toss his rock, which Mudd ducked. It soared through the passageway and into the ship. Sounds of protesting metal and the tinkle of broken glass responded from somewhere within.

"THIEF! ROBBER! SWINDLER!"

Another, small rock shot toward him, and he barely

slipped out of its way. As it bounced off the doorway, Mudd abruptly broke from the platform before he could be pinned in, showing unexpected speed as he raced toward the two watching starship officers. A hail of missiles pursued him.

"I surrender myself! I turn myself in!" He turned and waggled a warning finger at the advancing crowd as he dashed toward Kirk.

"Free will—mercy—I'm in protective custody now!"

"You forget, Harry!" yelled someone in the pursuing crowd, "Motherlode doesn't observe Federation law." This observation was punctuated by a fist-sized rock, which bounced off Mudd's lower back. He howled.

Kirk adjusted his communicator. At the same time, Spock took a couple of steps forward. Setting his phaser on high, he pointed it at the siliceous soil just behind Harry. The high-powered beam dug into the ground and threw up a blockading ridge of fused soil and glass in front of the oncoming miners.

Another stone sailed over the new blockade and hit Mudd in the back of his right leg. He yelped and continued on, half-running, half-limping, until he reached Kirk and Spock. He promptly took up a firm position facing his tormentors—from behind Kirk.

One of the humans had gained the top of the slick ridge and was reaching back to give the male ursinoid a hand over. The man with the projectile weapon was right behind, struggling to get a line on Mudd with the clumsy device.

But by then, Mudd, Kirk, and Spock were only half there, already fading from view as the transporter locked in and commenced dematerialization.

Harry Mudd continued to complain long and loud, but in transit stasis no one could hear him—not until they reformed in the transporter room of the *Enterprise*.

"Nicely done, Chief," Kirk complimented the man behind the transporter console. "Timing was ideal . . .

things were getting a little sticky." The transporter chief grinned, raised a hand deferentially.

"Easy enough, Captain, once I had Mudd's pattern set."

Blithely ignoring the fact that Kirk and Spock had just saved his life, Mudd continued his tirade.

"That was a meeching trick, Kirk! You've cost me my ship, my Rigellian—and if you think it was easy to train that half-intelligent lizard to play the siren, you know nothing of patience—everthing I own. Even the love crystals." He drew himself up and tried to appear threatening.

Instead, it made him look like something out of the *Mikado*. "I have a mind to contact my solicitor and sue you, personally."

"Fine," Kirk agreed. "I'll see you in court, Harry." Mudd glared at him as he stepped off the transporter platform. "Come along, now."

"Where are we going?"

"Where do people under arrest usually go, Harry?"

The trader bugged his eyes in outrage. "Why, Captain . . . ! Not to the brig? Surely you don't intend to lock me up on such unsubstantiated charges? To throw me behind a force field? To treat me like a common criminal?"

"Whatever you are, you're not common, Harry. But of course we aren't. We're going to put you in protective custody, that's all." He smiled.

Mudd bared his teeth and made a growling sound. The growl dissolved into a moan of seemingly real pain, the first honest verbalization, Kirk mused, that Mudd had probably made in weeks. The trader was pawing at his lower back, where the first thrown rock had struck.

"Spock."

"Yes, Captain?"

"Buzz Sick Bay. See that someone meets us in the

brig." Spock nodded, and Kirk directed their prisoner toward the elevator.

The *Enterprise*'s brig consisted of several small living areas and one large one, each divided by solid walls for privacy and fronting on the same corridor. All were unoccupied at the moment. Kirk walked Mudd into one of the compact apartments, directed him to sit down.

Spock arrived shortly thereafter, with nurse Christine Chapel. By now, Mudd was holding his lower back constantly, rocking in his seat and groaning theatrically.

"What's the trouble?" asked Chapel, eyeing the seated trader with distaste.

"Got hit in the back with a rock," Kirk informed her, before Mudd could detail his unending list of woes. "Nothing serious, I think."

"Nothing serious!" Mudd retorted in disbelief. "I've got a cracked vertebra, at the least."

"Oh, for heaven's sake, Harry, stop making such a fuss." Kirk shook his head. "The out-world free trader, the pioneer of the Federation, the advance guard of mankind." With representatives like Mudd, he couldn't help but wonder sometimes how humanity had gotten as far as it had.

Chapel, meanwhile, had lifted Mudd's tunic and was examining the broad back. There was a red bruise spreading on the lower portion, just above the belt-line.

She took out a small cylinder from the medikit satchel at her waist. It had a spray nozzle at one end and a simple trigger at the other. Setting it against the injured area, she depressed the activator.

There was a hiss, and a fine mist appeared around the nozzle as she moved the cylinder across the bruise. Judging by Mudd's exaggerated contortions, she might well have been using a sledge hammer.

"Minor bruise, Captain," she agreed, replacing the cylinder in her bag. "He'll live."

"Oh well, all news can't be good," Kirk mused dryly. Mudd shook his head in despair at this unfriendly observation and tucked his shirt back into his trousers.

"Tch, tch, Captain, such unwonted animosity from a man of your position."

"Believe me, Harry, I'm sorry you're here to hear it. If you hadn't forced yourself on us, I wouldn't be forcing my evaluations on you. How'd you get away, anyhow? I thought we'd left you on that robot world permanently."

A quivering finger shot skyward in a gesture of defiance. "Never underestimate the spirit of Harcourt Fenton Mudd! Those who make that fatal mistake soon learn to their detriment that all their—"

"Harry," Kirk interrupted patiently, "never mind the theatrics. How did you get away?"

Mudd's eyes sparkled. "Ah, the conception was true genius, Captain! An inspiration worthy of my unique talents in the field of sociological betterment.

"I introduced the concept of organized sports. It was glorious to behold—thousands of robot citizens participating, two teams locked in a hearty struggle for the honor of their home factories, their central computers. I then introduced the idea of formal betting, with all it's subtle variations, and—"

"I can imagine the rest," said Kirk, wincing at the image Mudd's words conjured up. The trader looked apologetic.

"Sadly, I forgot a small matter—the fact that I was dealing with automatons and not humans. They did not appreciate my exquisite and delicate refinements to the age-old logic of organized gambling."

"You mean cheating," Spock suggested helpfully.

"So I was, uh, compelled at an awkward moment to borrow a vehicle—"

"Steal a spaceship," Spock added once again. Mudd glared at the Vulcan.

"—and take my leave, only to find eventual haven

on Ilyria VI. A charming world, just recently granted full Federation status. An emerging culture eager for the blessings of Federation civiliztion. A people rich in those rare resources—friendship and innocence."

"Which you are an expert at mining—so you went and sold them the Starfleet Academy," Kirk finished. "Harry! That was a bit much, even for you."

"I was selling an idea," Mudd protested. "I offered no absolutes or promises."

"Not on paper or tape, anyway," Spock reminded him. "The . . . transaction netted you enough credits to get you to Sirius IX, in your stolen ship."

"Borrowed," reminded Mudd helpfully. "Where I discovered a great boon to intelligent life. Something humanoids have been searching for for thousands and thousands of years—and probably most aliens have, too. A real, chemically sound, and never-failing love potion!"

"Which you sold to at least a thousand inhabitants of Sirius IX," Kirk concluded, "who immediately became never-failingly ill from using it."

"Unfortunately, Captain, the spacecraft I sto—ah, borrowed, was not equipped for much in the way of extensive chemical analysis. So I was, sadly, unable to ascertain in advance that the love potion and biochemistry of my customers were mutually incompatible. So I proceeded, as is my wont, to do the honest thing, I left in haste, but not without first leaving behind all the credits I had made, to be refunded to my enthusiastic but physiologically deficient customers."

"Read—a bank on Sirius impounded your funds before you could withdraw them," Spock commented.

Mudd's smile was showing wear around the edges. "Really, Mr. Spock, I must confess that sometimes I do find your attention to trivial minutiae exhausting."

"Let us hope that the Peaceforcer court shows more interest when considering the same facts." Mudd made a mumbling sound deep in his throat.

"And so you came here," Kirk went on, "hoping to have better luck swindling honest miners—again, without worrying about any possible side effects your potion might have on *their* body chemistries."

Mudd's chin went out as he struck a noble pose. "Well, I have a surprise for you, Captain Kirk. Because, for once in my life, I've stumbled on something profitable as well as hon . . . sensible. The potion *works.*"

"As it did on Sirius IX?"

Mudd shrugged. "An unfortunate, unforeseeable accident of nature. An exception to the rule, I assure you." He leaned forward. "No, I can do better than assure you—I can *prove* it. If you will only permit me to procure a few samples from my ship . . ." He started to rise.

Kirk shook his head slowly. "Sorry, Harry." Taking a couple of steps backward, until he was standing in the corridor with Spock and Chapel, Kirk moved his hand over a switch set in the wall to his right.

Hidden instruments flicked on, and a mild hum became audible. Instantly, a thin but impenetrable force field had been erected between Mudd and the three starship officers.

The field itself—what one could see of it—looked something like heat distortion on a paved road on a hot day. As viewed through the field, the outline of Harry Mudd appeared to shift and waver slightly.

"Mr. Spock, you'll please prepare an official arrest report as soon as is convenient, giving all details including the use of the prohibited Rigellian hypnoid. And be sure to mention that Mr. Mudd voluntarily surrendered himself." Within the cell, Mudd mumbled a sarcastic "*Hah!*"

"Of course, Captain," Spock responded.

Kirk nodded, satisfied that he had heard the last of Harry Mudd until they reached Sector headquarters on Darius.

All men, even starship captains, dream.

"I'll be on the bridge if you need me, Mr. Spock," he finished, moving toward the elevator. Spock turned to look at the woman next to him.

"Nurse Chapel, I shall require a thorough medical report on the prisoner, to append to the arrest tape, assuring that he was healthy and in good condition when apprehended, no mind-warping techniques were used ... the usual."

"What about my back?" complained Mudd. "Good condition, my—"

Spock barely glanced back at him. "Note that Mr. Mudd suffered minor injury to his lower dorsal area while in the process of turning himself in."

She smiled up at him. "I'll note that, too, Mr. Spock." Her smile grew wider, warmer ... wishful. "I heard how you and the Captain managed it. I think you deserve congratulations for trapping him as neatly as you did." She started to lean forward, pursing her lips.

Spock drew away quickly, frowned. "I must remind you, Nurse Chapel, that intergender oral contact is not popular among Vulcans."

She looked disappointed, and embarrassed. "I ... I apologize, Mr. Spo—Commander."

Spock was unruffled. "It is not necessary. I am aware—indeed, I am constantly reminded—that emotional impulses may overcome humans at any point." He shook his head sadly. "How unfortunate for you."

"You don't know the half of it, Mr. Spock," she murmured, but so softly that no one could hear.

Mudd didn't have to, however. An astute observer of other beings, the look in her eyes was sufficient for him. He leaned forward on the combination lounge-bed and twirled one end of his mustache, trying not to look interested.

Well, well ... the universe is a bottomless bag of surprises, he reflected. *Most* intriguing.

"As to our capture of Mr. Mudd, you exaggerate," Spock continued formally. "Kindly see to it that your medical summary is more precise." He nodded curtly and left the brig area.

Chapel's stare followed him until the elevator doors had closed him away. Mudd did not have to be a telepath to know that she was interested in more than merely making sure he didn't stumble on his way out.

Mudd edged closer to the force-field "bar." When his skin began to tingle he knew he was right up against it. As Chapel continued to gaze down the corridor after the departed Spock, Mudd spoke casually.

"You're absolutely right, you know. I've dealt with a great many humanoids in my time, and your Mr. Spock is certainly a very attractive intelligence."

Wham! Mudd could almost see the mental portcullis slam shut in her head. Her voice was instantly the model of precision and bureaucratic indifference.

"An exceptional officer, yes. We're fortunate to be able to serve under him."

"But a trifle lacking in the warmer emotions, yes?" He smiled broadly when she jerked around to look at him. When she didn't say anything, he continued.

"Now you, nurse," and he rubbed his sore back as he chatted, "have a wonderful gift for healing the wounded. A considerable ability . . . a feminine, womanly touch.

"That's rare in the Federation today, and I don't mean just among Starfleet personnel. It's something I can appreciate. Most people, it seems, have grown so . . . well mechanical. You know.

"Anyway, I do appreciate it. And I think it's that sort of quality that could, well . . . what I'm trying to say is that I'd like to thank you." Balancing awkwardly on one foot, he commenced to reach down and remove his left boot. Chapel watched this operation uncertainly.

"Thank me . . . with a boot?"

"No, no, my dear. With this." And while she stared

he touched a hidden button at the back of the boot. A tiny spring sprang, and the heel clicked aside, revealing a small hollow compartment. It yielded an oblong, multicolored crystal that seemed to pulse with inner light—a neat cross between clear quartz and opal. A thick oily liquid rocked back and forth inside the transparent silicate.

Chapel found herself staring. "What is it?"

"My love potion." That brought her head up. "No, no," he said hastily. "It's not an illusion, not trickery, my dear Nurse Chapel. This is for real. Inside the crystal," and he tapped the specimen with a fingernail, "lies the power to create love . . . in another."

Chapel took a wary step backward. "Oh no you don't, Harry Mudd. I've heard about your potions. I don't believe you." She spun on her heel and started to leave. Mudd reached out, hurried down the short length of the cell with both hands pressed against the force field.

"But if it did," he implored, his voice rising desperately, "think about it, darlin'—Mr. Spock, in love with you. *Really* in love with you."

Arex looked back from his position at the navigation console to catch first Spock's eye, then Kirk's. "Something rather interesting here, sir."

The *Enterprise* was proceeding at high speed toward distant Darius on a normal exploration course. Now Arex started to slow . . . in case.

"Uncharted star system ahead."

"Put it on the screen, Mr. Arex." The latter flicked a switch. Instantly a tiny, far-off star system became visible on the main screen. An unspectacular blue-white sun boiled in its center.

"Increase magnification, Mr. Arex."

"Yes, sir." Arex did things with three controls at once. The picture leaped into clearer focus. Then he adjusted other dials, and the rest of the bridge saw the main object of interest—the blue-white's companion.

It was smaller, reddish-orange in color. Spock had been studying nonvisual information via the library computer's hooded viewer. Now he looked up and back at them.

"A standard binary system, Captain; but it appears to hold at least one Class-M planet. I think this is rare enough to warrant investigation." Kirk pondered a moment, then agreed.

"Yes, it is. All right, set us an orbit, Mr. Arex." The navigator began making requests of the incredibly complex piloting system. Kirk stared at the viewscreen as they began to edge into the double-star family.

The growing blue-white sun seemed to throb with light, pulse and sparkle, sparkle and flame and . . .

. . . Sparkle hypnotically as Mudd twirled the crystal, back and forth and around and back in his hands like a top on a string. Nurse Chapel stared at it, fascinated, entranced. She also held a hand phaser aimed squarely at Harry's midsection.

"If it did work," she said slowly, "which is quite absurd, would it . . . ?"

"It's so simple, my dear. Nothing to it. Yes, it would."

"How does it work—theoretically, I mean."

"Nothing easier and less obvious," Mudd continued smoothly, still twirling, spinning, and shifting the crystal. "You merely crush the crystal and allow the liquid a second or two to sink into your skin. The hands are best. Then simply touch another person—*the* other person."

"And it creates love? Mudd, that's ridiculous."

"Isn't all love ridiculous?" he argued philosophically. "But you are wrong, darlin'—the crystals are infallible. One touch from a liquid-kissed hand evokes undying friendship among men, or women. But between members of the opposite sex, you get love. The real thing, guaranteed." He held the crystal closer to the force-field.

"Harry Mudd's love crystals could generate passion in a block of granite. Now your Mr. Spock—he's something of a block of granite, isn't he?" Mudd tossed the crystal from hand to hand.

"But naturally, you're skeptical." Taking a couple of steps back into the cell, he didn't miss how her gaze followed the crystal as it moved from palm to palm.

"Now you can appreciate a unique bit of chemistry like this, Christine. You're not only a beautiful woman, you're a scientist. Why, you're practically a physician yourself, in every way but on parchment. I urge you, take this love crystal as my gift of gratitude to you. For your medical ministrations and your comforting hands.

"I assure you, it can't harm you. Even Captain Kirk would tell you that. Why don't you ask him?"

"Ask . . . ? No . . . no, I don't think that's necessary. I mean, there's no need to bother the Captain with . . ." She stopped, flustered, and tried another tack. "It can't harm me? Then what about those people on Sirius IX?"

"Ah, you've heard of that," he commented disappointedly. "No matter. They only became slightly ill. There were no serious sicknesses. You can check that, too, if you wish. But human biochemistry should react to it most favorably. And Vulcan." He tried to appear disinterested.

"Look on it as an experiment." He extended the hand holding the crystal toward her, pulled it back when the force-field firmly rejected it, and chuckled good-naturedly.

"Sorry—forgot, for a minute."

"Not that I believe any of this rubbish," she muttered, but without meeting his eyes. "I suppose it wouldn't hurt to analyze the effects."

"Of course not!" He grinned widely.

She hesitated a last minute, then hefted the phaser tightly and reached for the wall-field control. The force-field vanished. Mudd could tell it was gone because the outline of Chapel no longer rippled.

Smiling, he made a courtly bow, noticing as he did so that the hand holding the phaser never wavered. He extended the crystals, careful not to make any sudden movement.

She took it gingerly, handling it like a fusion bomb. Which, in a sense, it was. Keeping the phaser on Mudd, she held it up to the light. Inside, the liquid refracted light, sending it out in myriad flashes every time the crystal shifted . . .

VII

One new image after another flashed across the *Enterprise*'s bridge viewscreen as her automatic cameras and recorders scanned the world below. Panoramas alternated with sequential closeups, building a composite picture of the surface.

Basically it was a dry world, a desert planet. Seemingly endless plains of fine sand, deep as oceans in spots, were interrupted only by occasional upthrusts of naked, worn, black rock that registered amazing hardness on the ship's sensors. It would have to be, to withstand the gargantuan dust storms that must everlastingly abrade the skin of the uninhabited globe. The ship's tracking computer finally settled on a medium telescopic view of an area somewhere beneath them.

Sunset there, second sunset, with the blue-white sun already down and the reddish binary turning the sand the color of dried blood. Long shadows turned the surface the color of coal behind the few protruding spires.

The *Enterprise* slid inside the orbit of the planet's single, insignificant moon as Kirk activated the log.

"Ship's Log, Stardate 5514.6.

"We have located and made preliminary scan of a hitherto unidentified binary system with one marginally habitable world. Preparations are now underway for first advanced survey. Second advanced survey with actual landing party will probably not be carried out this trip, unless some unexpected new factor dictates in its favor."

And from the look of that dead, motionless surface,

Kirk expected nothing in the way of startling developments. He looked up from the log mike.

"Mr. Spock, have you got those preliminary statistics ready?"

"Here, Captain." Kirk joined his first officer at the library computer. A small screen was playing back the initial probe and sensor reports from their first, fast orbit around the planet's equator. All were neatly correlated and broken down to essential components.

The *Enterprise*'s planetary detection equipment took a world apart, reduced it to a series of figures that were taken into the library computer. There the ship's brain sorted them out, packed them together, and generally translated them into terms a well-educated Starfleet officer could comprehend.

Arex remained at the helm, keeping a close check on their position to insure that their orbit wasn't varying, while M'ress continued her search via communications equipment for any signs of intelligent life. If any such existed in the sandpit below them, they weren't very talkative. So far she'd found nothing, not even a hint of a primitive crystal set.

All these bits and pieces linked up with the computer's preliminary evaluations. This was no world to nourish intelligent life.

"Parking orbit holding, Captain," said Arex over a shoulder. "All weapon's systems on defensive standby." Spock had returned to his station and was again studying the computer readouts for the latest information.

"No evidence of even a primitive society, Captain, though there are signs of standard organic forms—a normal dry-planet ecology."

"Reasonable," Kirk murmured idly, staring at the screen. They wouldn't be here terribly long, then. A subsequent expedition could study what little this world had to offer at some future date. He saw no reason to tie up the *Enterprise* in a painstaking study of local flora and fauna.

"Atmosphere at surface, eight hundred millibars," the science officer continued. "Gravity, one point two. Mean temperature—hot, but within Class-M limits. Seasonal fluctuation . . ."

Chapel finally lowered the crystal and returned her attention to Harry Mudd. "I'll let you know the results of my analysis. It'll be thorough, I assure you."

"But the crystal is so sensitive, my dear. However carefully executed, laboratory tests would probably destroy it. Once broken, it's completely useless. And it's the only one I have left." He smiled, and his tone became urgent.

"Why not try it out the way it's meant to be tried?"

"No," Chapel protested—weakly, he thought. "I don't think I ought . . ."

"Darlin', consider! If it does what I say it does—and it does," he paused significantly, "Spock will be yours forever. And there are no side effects, nothing to show that it wasn't the real thing."

She still hesitated, considering, and finally came to a decision. She nodded and slipped the hand phaser back onto her belt. "I just break the crystal and let the liquid sink into my skin?"

Mudd smiled. "And then touch him."

Chapel raised the crystal once again, staring into its crystalline depths, then she abruptly closed her fist on it. There was a faint, ethereal pop, like the shriek of some miniscule animal as the crystal turned to powder. The oily liquid now covered her palm.

She brought both hands together and rubbed it into them. For good measure she touched a bit of it to her cheeks. Hands and face dried rapidly as the alien substance either sank into her pores or evaporated.

Suddenly she began to sway dizzily, gasping for air, and sank quickly to the floor in a half faint.

"What is it?" she stammered, crouching on her knees and putting both hands to her head. "What's happening?"

Mudd casually stepped over the boundary of the now deactivated force-screen and bent over her. "Nothin' at all, darlin'. A temporary reaction engendered by absorbing the potion. It'll pass right away."

As he spoke, he gently took the hand phaser from her belt. A moment's further search turned up a thin strip of plastic, which he also pocketed.

Chapel struggled to get to her feet, wobbled, and had to steady herself with a hand on the deck. Her vision was starting to clear.

"Here, darlin' . . . let me give you a hand." He got an arm under hers and lifted, careful not to touch her where the liquid had been applied.

"I . . . I feel better, I think."

"Of course, didn't I tell you it would be over fast?" She was sweating and shaking her head, still slightly dazed from the strange aftereffects of the drug.

Several things were troubling her, but the fog in her mind seemed to solidify around them rather than clear. Wait a minute . . . one of them, at least, was staring back at her.

"You . . . you should be in the brig, Harry."

"Why so I should," Mudd observed amiably. He took a couple of steps backward until he was standing in the cell again. Chapel hit the force-field activator on the wall. She had to repeat the gesture, missing badly on her first try. Once again Mudd's outline wavered as the distorting field appeared between them. But now she was sure that the waver *was* in the field . . . not in her suddenly cleared mind.

"Why don't you, ah, go find Spock?" he suggested. "The liquid won't stay potent forever, you know."

"Yes," she muttered, then repeated more firmly, "Yes . . . I'll do that." She headed up the corridor.

Mudd paced quietly around in his cell for several

minutes, inspecting it from all angles. After he was sure
the elevator had started on its way, he reached into a
pocket and brought out the hand phaser. A careful ad-
justment of the aperture to what he estimated would be
the minimum necessary setting, and he pressed the trigger.

There was a flash, the beam of energy contacted the
minimal force-shield, and it winked out. Mudd grunted
his satisfaction and repocketed the phaser. Smiling and
whistling happily, he strolled out of the cell and headed
for the elevator.

Mudd got off on a little-frequented service deck. He
needed a quiet place, a temporary refuge, and the service area seemed the best place to find it.

Walking down the main corridor, he checked room
after room. Anything that showed recent signs of visita-
tion, he skipped. Likewise he bypassed any chamber
containing material that might be needed for the min-
ute-to-minute operation of the starship.

Finally, he located a near-empty storage room that
also possessed an inside lock. This would do for a few
hours. He did not expect to be there long.

Sitting down on a canister marked EMERGENCY
LUBRICATION SUPPLY and using a big metal crate
for a workbench, he took out the thin, flat strip of plastic that he had taken from a pouch at Nurse Chapel's
waist. After setting it carefully on the crate, he reached
for his boot. The heel clicked aside and yielded up a
tiny packet of miniature tools.

Humming to himself and working deftly but quickly,
he first erased Nurse Chapel's identifying picture from
the Starfleet Identity Card. From the packet he produced a tiny, flat piece of metal about the size of his
thumbnail. Slipping it delicately over the now gleaming
blank space on the card, he pressed down on it with his
thumb. There was a slight click.

When he let off the pressure and slid the tiny square

aside, it was his own smiling visage that beamed back up at him from the card.

He put the subminiature tridee duplicator aside and started in on the card with several of the other tiny tools. It would take some time and precision work to erase all Chapel's identification and replace it with his own.

The private quarters of the *Enterprise*'s first officer were much like their tenant—ordered, reasoned, logical. A place for everything and everything in its place. Even the art on the walls reflected a somber regularity of composition much like the man who had purchased it.

Just now that man was working at the large desk which dominated the main room. Spock was running through information being displayed on the readout screen of the desk's own computer annex. The door chime sounded once. He spoke without looking up.

"Come."

Chapel entered, moved to stand next to him. She was carrying a flat microtape cassette in one hand and several other things in her mind. All were intended for Spock.

Trying not to shake, Chapel stood patiently behind Spock while the desk computer hummed and clicked. Finally, he paused in his work, turned to look up at her.

"Yes, what is it, Nurse?"

"I brought the medical summary for the arrest report, Mr. Spock—the one you asked for?"

"Yes. Thank you, Chapel." He swiveled in his chair, reaching out for the microtape cassette. As he did so, she took a step forward and stumbled awkwardly, falling into his lap.

The startled Spock caught her reflexively. She clutched at him, managing to effect a good deal of physical contact. He looked at her uncertainly.

"Sorry, sir," she apologized, feigning surprise. She paused expectantly, still resting in his arms. Spock sat still, waiting for her to get up. When it became apparent that, for unknown reasons, she wasn't going to move, he rose himself and deposited her on her feet.

"Are you injured, or something, Nurse Chapel?" He couldn't keep the irritation out of his tone, though his expression remained neutral, as always.

"No, I'm fine," she replied, in a voice that indicated she was anything but.

Vulcans have several interesting abilities and senses that humans do not. Sensing sudden rises in blood pressure, however, was not among them.

"Are *you* feeling all right?" she asked hopefully.

"Perfectly normal." He picked the cassette off the desk. "I will append the summary to the report." He waited. When she didn't say thank you, good-bye, or anything else, he shrugged ever so slightly and sat back down at the annex, resuming his work.

Several minutes passed before he noticed that she was still standing behind him. Now he was concerned instead of irritated.

"Was there something else, Nurse?"

Chapel stuttered, one hand moving out to him and hurriedly pulling back. "Wouldn't ... wouldn't you like me to ... stay? To help you?"

"I am managing quite easily by myself, Nurse Chapel. For you to stay would be unnecessary, duplicative, and illogical. Do you not see this?"

"Yes," she whispered. Then her voice turned tight, controlled. "Yes—it'd be damn stupid, in fact." She spun on a heel and marched from the room.

For a minute Spock continued to stare after her, puzzled. Her actions seemed more than normally ... human. Then he shook his head—no matter how long he lived and worked among humans he would never fully understand them—and returned to his work.

Chapel had some work to do, too. She ignored the

casual greetings of fellow crewmembers as she moved down several corridors on her way to the brig, turning over in her mind the various indignities, both verbal and physical, she intended to subject one Harry Mudd to.

Eventually, the single security elevator deposited her in the *Enterprise*'s security corridor. She was speaking before she reached the cell.

"All right now, Harry Mudd. You're in for it, you illegitimate, swindling . . ."

She came abreast of the cell, glared in—and came up short, gaping. No fluttering, apprehensive outline greeted her. Not even a smiling, unwavering one. The force-field barrier was truly off, and the cell itself absolutely empty.

She whirled quickly, thinking perhaps he had somehow managed to slip out and even now was preparing to jump her. Her hand went to her belt for her phaser and clutched nothing but fabric. It shifted, moved up to her head where, she was beginning to think, it might also contact nothing.

The dizzy spell—aftereffects—over quickly. She glanced down at her waist belt as if the hoped-for phaser might somehow respond to visual if not tactile identification. No luck. It wasn't there.

"Oh no," she muttered softly. Then she was running for the elevator.

SHUTTLECRAFT BAY—AUTHORIZED PERSONNEL ONLY

Mudd examined with pleasure the boldly printed words on the door blocking his way. Then he moved to a small blank screen set in the wall to one side and stood in front of it.

Taking a deep breath, he slipped his newly modified identification card into the slot beneath the screen. If anyone in ship security decided to make a routine check on this shuttle-bay entry it would all be up for him—he didn't look even faintly like Christine Chapel. But the screen only flared once, with white light, as the automatics processed the visitor. There was a brief wait that seemed to Mudd to last only one or two millennia, then a green light winked on beneath the screen. A hum, and the door slid obediently aside. Taking the card out of the slot, Mudd released his breath and hurried through. He paused inside as the door slid shut behind him.

The shuttlecraft hangar was filled with the normal complement of offship Starfleet vehicles. There was a small, superfast scout ship, a heavily armored landing vehicle for worlds with surfaces even more inhospitable than the one rumored to be revolving beneath them, and a hovercraft for those planets with totally antagonistic surfaces, or even none at all.

There were also several light planetary atmosphere fliers, and three compact shuttlecraft themselves. He rubbed his hands together and wished he could let out with a really good bellow of laughter, but someone might have a mike open someplace. So he contented himself with the thought.

Harry Mudd, triumphant again!

He moved at a fast walk toward the waiting vessels.

Unaware that the subject of his arrest report was preparing to invalidate same, Spock had switched off the small desk computer annex and was now concluding that report, dictating into a tiny hand recorder.

"... and appended hereto is a medical summary and evaluation of the prisoner with statement by Nurse Christine Chapel ..." He stopped abruptly, drew a deep, startled breath.

Broke into a wide smile. It was fortunate he didn't happen to be gazing into a mirror just then. The shock might have rendered him unconscious.

He blinked, coughed. The smile vanished as abruptly

as it had appeared. Facial muscles unused to the expression were protesting angrily. He cleared his throat again, resumed dictating.

"Uh . . . Nurse . . . Chapel . . . summary appen—"

Again the sharp hesitation, but this time astonished hands fluttered to his upcurved lips. He shook his head violently, then scrambled to his feet, shoving back the chair like a man suddenly possessed—which was exactly the case.

"Christine . . . Chap-el." The last syllable trailed off in a deep, heaving sigh. "Dear, lovely Christine." He sighed again, and his face contorted in horror. He stumbled into the desk, jerked away as though it had transformed itself into a monstrous, four-legged spider.

"Christine—" A sharp pain hit him, as if someone was pounding with steady rhythm on his stomach.

Chapel would have recognized the sensation.

It ought to be fully fueled, ready for an extended mission at any time. Mudd examined the long-range scoutship lovingly. The onboard computer, a miniature of the one that ran the *Enterprise*, could draw on its parent machinery for information. Before anyone caught on, it should be able to give him the ship's current position, accept his fast course setting—for Ilyria, say—and put him instantly out of detector range.

Of course, the *Enterprise* could easily track and overtake him—if anyone noticed his departure, that is. There were steps he could take to insure that no one would. All he needed was five minutes at the scoutship's nominal but still impressive warp-drive, and he would be over the hill and far away before—

Something hit him hard on the back of the neck. Everything went space-dark for a time, space flecked with an appreciable number of stars . . . though not of solar magnitude.

When his vision cleared, his eyes presented him with an extreme close-up view of the deck. Instinctively one hand went up and back to caress his aching neck. He grimaced when it touched. A slow heave and he rolled himself over, then almost wished he hadn't. In its own innocent way, the deck was a preferable view.

Christine Chapel, looking very unlike an angel of mercy at the moment, reached down and scooped up the hand phaser that had fallen from Harry's belt. She pointed it at an indelicate portion of his anatomy.

"I've come to collect on your guarantee, Mr. Mudd."

So close—he'd come so close! He grumbled in frustration as he climbed to his feet.

No one on the bridge happened to be scanning the shuttle bay, so Kirk, Arex, M'ress, and Scott continued to be unaware of the play being acted out below.

McCoy was at Spock's vacant library computer station, indulging himself in some minor research of a nonmedical nature. Everyone else was at his station— calm, relaxed. No one glanced up right away when the elevator doors slid back, and Spock stepped onto the bridge.

He moved forward, found himself pausing. He swallowed nervously. But contrary to what surely must be obvious, no one stared at him, no one showed that anything unusual was taking place. No one noticed his confusion.

They noticed the difference in his voice, however. And they all turned at the first words.

"Captain . . ." He hesitated. "Doctor, I believe I require medical attention." McCoy's eyes widened slightly. "I . . . wish to report a number of . . . of very strange . . . emotions.

"*What?*" The reaction burst simultaneously from Kirk and McCoy. M'ress and Arex just stared.

In the Shuttle Bay, Mudd had regained his feet and was now edging nervously along the wall behind the scout ship, moving toward a nearby complex of bay machinery. Every so often, the grim-faced Chapel would make jabbing motions at him with the phaser as she pursued. Or she would jerk down on it with a finger, just missing the trigger.

Each time she did so, Mudd—who was sweating heavily, and not from the exertion of walking—would give a little start and his high-powered smile would lose a little more voltage.

"Ah, you are implying, darlin', that the potion wasn't completely successful?" Chapel laughed harshly.

"That depends on the point of view, I suppose. Oh, it was beautiful, Harry. I made a thorough fool of myself. I'm sure you're sorry you missed it. But don't worry—what I'm going to do to you will be even funnier." Somehow, to Mudd, the promise seemed lacking in humor.

"But you know how cold Vulcans are," he reminded quickly. "Possibly," and he shook a finger at her as she jabbed with the phaser again, "the reaction is slightly delayed, the potion may need a few more minutes to take effect. After all, with such a reluctant subject as Spock . . ."

She shook her head sadly. "And I had such hopes. But you're the same foul-mouthed fraud you've always been, Harry. I don't know what came over me that would let me believe you, even for a moment. After all the people you've swindled—" Once again the muzzle of the phaser came up.

"Now, nobody's perfect," Mudd hurried to remind her. "And I fell in with bad companions at an early age. Leave us not act rashly, my dear. No need to do something now for which we'll be sorry later."

"Oh, don't worry, Harry. I won't be—I won't be." He started to tremble, and she clucked her tongue in disgust. "Don't panic, you sniveling coward."

"I can't help it—that is a habit that seems to affect all us sniveling cowards."

"Harry, this phaser's only set on stun. And I think

we've gone about far enough." They had backed right
into the complex of machinery. There was an intercom
screen nearby for the use of any technicians who might
be working on the complex. It was time to end the
game.

"Activate the intercom, Harry."

"Now wait a minute, luv," he cautioned brightly, a
suggestive cloud appearing in his head. "I have a
thought—"

He continued to move backward along the wall, ever
deeper into the complex. There was a printed legend on
the towering tank he was backing up to.

AIR REGENERATION AND DISTRIBUTION

He reached into his pocket, jerked his arm, and produced a ripping sound. Christine looked at him curiously. When he withdrew his hand, he held several fine
large love crystals, taken from the lining of his pants.

"Try another. I promise you, they'll work. Spock
will be so in love with you he'll—"

"Stop it!" she yelled angrily, waving the phaser.

As soon as the compact weapon was no longer
pointed at him, Mudd jumped to one side and threw
the crystals, whooping and diving at her. The awkwardly thrown handful soared high, to shatter well
overhead near an open grid.

Taken by surprise by his war-yell and charge, Christine stumbled backward, firing awkwardly and
bumping against the alarm button set under the intercom screen. The phaser blast missed; the wide beam
streaking over the lunging trader's shoulder to scorch
the metal tower behind him.

Somewhere a siren screamed.

Neither of them, of course, bothered to look upward—they were otherwise occupied—upward, to
where the powdered crystal and evaporating liquid
were sucked efficiently into the grid by hidden fans.

Harry Mudd was not a small man. He slammed into
Chapel hard, his shoulder striking the arm with the

phaser. The arm jerked up and back, the phaser discharged again, and the stun-beam caught her in the throat. She sagged instantly into his reluctant arms.

"By the sacred thumbs of Hnisto!" He shifted his feet, lifted her upright. "Sorry Christine, darlin'—but I'm afraid I'm going to need a hostage now. Why couldn't you have let me leave quietly, without going and alerting the whole ship?"

At the same time, he was looking around the bay, toward the scoutship again, considering furiously. With the alarm ringing, but not pinpointed, the brig would be one of the first places automatically checked. The scout looked fast, but without his five-minute lead it would never outrun or outmaneuver the *Enterprise*.

But there was a planet beneath them. Often, a finite world proved a better hiding place than infinite space. But not the scoutcraft, no . . . he headed toward the armored landing vehicle, settling the inert Christine over one shoulder. They'd have a hard time prying him out of *that*.

Spock's confession of deep troubles and subsequent expressions of shock and surprise were interrupted by the alarm. A multitude of questions forgotten, everyone rushed to emergency stations. M'ress cut off the squalling alarm. Arex checked the security panels and reported back.

"It's not a damage alarm, sir. No sign of hostile craft in the immediate vicinity—here it is. Internal security —shuttlecraft bay."

"Give us some visual, Mr. Arex," instructed Kirk calmly. The navigator activated a switch, and everyone looked to the left as a small viewscreen set over the library-science station lit up. It showed the shuttlecraft bay, the ships within, but no sign of anything worthy of an alarm.

"Pan it," Kirk said curtly. The camera began to move. "Hold it, Mr. Arex." Two figures had come into view, one apparently carrying the others unmoving form.

Everyone recognized Mudd's portly shape instantly, but the identity of his limp burden remained indistinct until the head lolled loosely backward.

"Mudd!" Spock shouted passionately. "And he has Christine. She's in danger . . . my belov—" His eyes suddenly widened in horror, and both eyebrows tried to crawl up his forehead and hide in his hair.

"Interesting . . . reactions . . ." he mumbled.

McCoy's jaw opened much wider than normal, but for a change, nothing came forth. Engineer Scott's hand slipped and nearly reversed the Enterprise's artificial gravity before he caught himself. M'ress murmured a meow of puzzlement, while Arex let out a long, low whistle.

"Close Shuttle Bay doors," Kirk finally managed to stammer, noticing that the giant panels in the bay were parting. Arex worked at his controls, turned back worriedly.

"Negative, Captain. Mudd has engaged the landing engines on the armored lander. Shuttle Bay doors will not close while a craft is exiting."

Of course they wouldn't. Spock's outburst and the subsequent shock had delayed his reactions a few seconds too long. The emergency override was designed to prevent the massive doors from accidentally closing on a departing ship once they were engaged.

"Mudd's decided he's got a better chance by going planetside, then," Kirk observed. "He can't make enough speed to lose us, so he's going to try and hide until we get bored and go away. Then he'll make for the nearest inhabited world . . . slowly, but he'll get there. And we can't wait here forever to find him."

"We can't wait at all," came the yell from the library computer station. "Not while he's got my Christine!"

"We must go after them, Captain." Spock was haranguing Kirk. "I'll lead a landing party."

McCoy moved toward the library computer station, his gaze never leaving the science officer. "Spock, you're obviously not yourself—maybe a little rest."

"Captain," he said, with an uncharacteristically angry glance at McCoy, "I insist on going." His eyes went to the viewscreen, which showed only the vague, rust-red surface of the planet below.

"Christine ... Christine Chapel. I can't stand the thought of any danger to her, to the woman I love."

If there had been surprise and shock on the bridge before, everyone now registered a state of total stupefaction. All attention focused on the commanding figure of Spock.

"Love?" a gawking Kirk managed to blurt.

"Spock?" McCoy managed to get a great deal into the mere mention of the first officer's name.

Seemingly unaware of the astounded reactions he had provoked, the first officer of the *Enterprise* smiled, a distant dreamy smile that on anyone else would have seemed charming—but on him gave hints of the most nefarious possibilities.

"Yes, I want to protect her. I must hold her in my arms." A cloud seemed to fall across his face, and he halted in mid-sentence as if aghast at what he'd been saying. For a moment his expression tightened and he was the old Spock.

But only for a moment. Then he slumped into another smile. Kirk stared at him, worried.

"Ordinarily I wouldn't consider an immediate pursuit ... not until our sensors have locked Mudd in. We might even be able to pull him back via transporter. But if you absolutely insist on going down there yourself ..."

"I do."

"Then I'll transport down with you," Kirk finished, with a sigh.

"Excellent. We have no time to waste, Captain." He spun and moved for the elevator. Kirk left the command chair and started to follow, but McCoy intercepted him.

"Jim ... do you think this is wise? In his present, unhealthy condition?"

"I wouldn't say it was so unhealthy, Bones. Unusual for Spock, certainly, but unhealthy ... ? I don't know."

"Well I do, Jim. It's a sign of abnormality—completely unnatural for him. Love among Vulcans is more, well, more constrained than this."

"All right," Kirk nodded in agreement. "I'll go along with that. *You* try and stop him."

McCoy started to reply, found he didn't have one. "I see what you mean."

"It's better we don't try to restrain him—and I'll be with him." He turned. "Mr. Scott, you're in command till I return."

"Aye, sir." The chief engineer moved to the command chair as Kirk and McCoy exited in pursuit of Spock.

Astonished silence lingered on the bridge following the departure of the three senior officers.

"Spock ..." Scott finally muttered. "Spock ... in love? What do you suppose could have caused a thing like that?"

"I can't begin to imagine," murmured M'ress. She was about to offer additional comment when something faint and aromatic crossed her nostrils. She sniffed. There was a faint hissing sound that accompanied the strange odor. No one else noticed it, none of them being as sensitive as M'ress. And even she failed to detect the slight vapor, nearly invisible, puffing from one of the air vents.

Now the smell was strong enough for Scott to notice, too. He took a deep, curious whiff ... and let his face relax in a broad, easy smile. "In ... love."

M'ress shook her head, the ruff on the back of her neck bristling slightly. Then she began to purr softly at nothing in particular. In fact, the attitude of everyone left on the bridge appeared to grow . . . contented.

Spock was waiting for them in the corridor. "Please, Captain. We cannot spare time for dawdling."

McCoy made a last plea. "I wish you'd let me run some tests on you first, Spock. You're not well."

"On the contrary, Doctor, I've never felt quite so alive in my life. Captain?" Kirk shrugged, and the two officers headed for the transporter room. McCoy had been intercepted by a yeoman from security and remained behind engaged in deep discussion with her.

Spock and Kirk entered the transporter room together. Chief Kyle glanced up easily at their arrival, did a double take at the wild look in Spock's eyes.

Kirk moved quickly to him. "Captain, I—" Kyle broke off, continuing to stare at the nervously pacing first officer. He whispered, "What's with Mr.—"

"No time for explanations now, Chief. I'll tell you later . . . I hope. Have you been tracking the lander that left just a few minutes ago?"

"Yes, sir. Standard emergency procedure, but . . . ?"

"Where are they now?"

"Close to touch-down—right near the surface, I'd guess."

"Okay, put Mr. Spock and myself down next to it."

"As you wish, sir." Kyle quieted, engaged in keeping close track of the landing craft while Spock continued his pacing. If they could set down just as Mudd was making up his mind which way to jump . . .

Finally, unable to stand it any longer, Spock walked over to look across the transporter console at Kyle. "If he's harmed one hair on her beautiful, sensitive head—"

If the first officer's intention was to spur the transporter chief to further effort, it had the opposite effect. Kyle's hands fluttered weakly over the controls as he stared at the first with an expression of amazement.

"Mr. Spock, I . . ."

But Spock had whirled and stalked into the transporter alcove. He was waiting impatiently on one of the disks. It was several seconds before Kyle could recover from the brief, if devastating, verbal onslaught and resume tracking the landing craft. And he still had setdown coordinates to compute.

He wanted to question Kirk further, but was interrupted by the soft closing of portal as McCoy joined them.

"What is it, Bones?" the Captain asked.

"A search party found this in the shuttlecraft bay. One of the yeomen thought a chemical analysis might be in order, so she brought it to me. It wasn't necessary."

He held out his open hand. A familiar glittering shape rested there. Kirk took it, held it up to the overhead light and inspected it closely. As he was doing so, his gaze passed over to the waiting, impatient Spock.

"One of Harry Mudd's so-called love crystals, broken." And understanding suddenly dawned.

"Jim, one of the party also found traces of pulverized crystal near one of the recirculation grids. I'd guess from the amount of residue that one or more of these things was broken against it. Nothing's happened so far, but I'm going to have the purification system purged, anyway.

"Good idea, Bones. That should handle any latent effects."

"I hope so, Jim. I passed several of the crew in the corridors, and some of them are looking mighty strange."

"For Vulcan's sake," came Spock's pleading voice, "let us hurry, Captain."

"Easy, Spock," Kirk replied soothingly. "We can't go anywhere till we know where Mudd has set down." His stare lingered a moment on the troubled first officer before returning to McCoy.

"Check it out, Bones. And send me an immediate report if it looks like there might be trouble." McCoy nodded and left the room. Kirk moved to step into the transporter alcove, taking a disk next to Spock.

The same landing coordinates Kyle was computing were being studied on the bridge. Lt. M'ress had taken over Spock's library station, and Scott was standing next to her. She was staring into the hooded viewer.

"Sensors indicate Mudd has landed on the surface." She depressed a couple of levers in combination. "Confirming coordinates sent to transporter room."

Scott laughed quietly. "And the captain's in transports about it—together with our ever-lovin' Mr. Spock." He chuckled again. M'ress found herself laughing with him, an irregular mewing sound.

She stood up, turned away from the hooded viewer, and reached out with one paw. Tiny clipped claws sprouted silently. Hesitantly, then with more conviction, she ran the sharp hooks along his neck and shoulders.

"It's ... funny. I hadn't rrealized it beforre, but you'rre funny. And verry attrractive forr a human, Mr. Scott." He laughed again and smiled warmly back at her.

"Hey, easy, lass ... that tickles."

She purred and moved a little closer ...

VIII

It was day on the new world. Both suns were up, and the light beat at the sand like a hammer. A towering cliff of sheer, jet-black rock rose out of the dunes. It was perhaps twenty meters high, slightly rounded and shining.

Twin shadows lanced out in different directions. Another weird double shadow formed, shifting and sharp against the ground, as the heavy landing craft made its gentle touch-down. It squatted silently in the dead air like a great ugly beetle.

All was still; nothing moved for several long minutes. Then a small dark cavity appeared in one side of the beetle and two tiny figures exited. They were immediately joined by four shadows.

"They'll find you soon enough, my little poppin," said Mudd. The temperature, thanks to the planet's distance from the twin suns, was not unbearable, and the atmosphere cut down enough on the radiation so that anyone caught unprotected in the sun would not find himself neatly toasted before lunch. But without shelter, a human would tan mighty fast on this world.

"You'll be quite safe," he insisted, "and by the time you are rescued I'll be long gone."

"Gone where," Chapel asked sardonically, looking around. "This planet's one big desert, deserted."

"There's always an opportunity for an ingenious man," he told her thoughtfully. "Better free on a desert than safe in a brig. Once, on Omega VII, I turned a handsome profit selling the natives their own oceans."

Nurse Chapel could not decide whether this typically

132

outrageous claim was partly truthful or pure fabrication. Certainly it was no more absurd than her present situation.

"Well if you're thinking of selling any locals these deserts, you'd better abandon it, Harry. We've detected no traces of intelligent life here."

"Then you can relax, eh?" Mudd said expansively, "since that means there's no danger."

There was a concerned note in her voice. "I said no *intelli*gent life. We did, I hear, find traces of nonsentient organic forms."

Mudd grunted. "It hardly looks like you'll be overwhelmed in the short time you'll be waiting for pickup, darlin'," He gestured around them and for the first time they both took a long look at their place of planetfall.

The landscape that greeted this survey had not been designed to please human desires. There were occasional clusters of towering black stone, some scrubby vegetation thrown in as an afterthought by an uncaring nature—and oceans, oceans of sand. Brown sand, reddish sand, yellow and black sand. There was nothing else.

She turned back to him. "You're *not* leaving me alone in this?"

"Don't worry, darlin'. We'll get you set up first class. No, don't bother to thank me."

"I hadn't planned on it," she replied, eyeing the phaser which Mudd held with seeming unconcern in one hand. If she could trip him and made a grab for it before they went back inside the lander . . .

Mudd wasn't quite *that* relaxed, however. "Ah, ah . . . naughty thoughts, Christine." He waved a warning finger at her and took a wary step backward, then gestured up the ramp and made a little bow.

She sighed, resigned. It appeared that she was going to be the ignominious subject of a rescue from the *En-*

terprise, while Mudd made good his escape. And he might, at that.

If Mudd could find a deep cave, he could hide the lander. And with its power turned off, the tiny block of metal would be practically invisible to the *Enterprise*'s sensors. His only problem then would be confusing the ship's life sensors, and Chapel did not doubt that someone as resourceful as Harry Mudd would find a way to manage that.

This escapade surely would not look good on her record.

Mudd left the hatch door open behind them, enjoying the influx of fresh air after days in space. He wasn't worried about Chapel escaping—where would she escape to?

The first low ridge of black rocks lay about a half a kilometer from the landing craft. If either of them had been looking in that direction just now, they might have noticed a faint movement about two-thirds of the way up the front of the ridge.

Surely it was a trick of the light from the double suns. Or perhaps a slight rockfall. But the rippled black surface moved again. It wasn't a trick of light, nor a fall of small rocks, but rather a wholly different and unbelievable phenomenon. Part of the black "rock" slid upward, like a massive door. The smooth, glassy surface revealed beneath exhibited a moisture that had nothing to do with hidden springs. The surface moved again, downward, as the massive eye inclined to stare at the tiny landing craft.

"I've got 'em pinned, Captain. No mistake, they've set down. And according to sensors Mudd's staying in place for a few minutes, anyway. His engines are off." Kyle was too busy to notice the slight fragrant aroma that had drifted into the room, and his voice covered the hiss from an overhead ventilation grid.

"Ready to transport down."

"Ready," both Kirk and Spock acknowledged. A high, musical whine filled the transporter chamber. Two chromatic columns of light appropriated the figures of the two officers as Kyle moved levers upward.

One of the figures seemed to sniff uncertainly at the air just before he was effectively dematerialized. Kyle brought the levers down sharply, and the electronic cadence vanished.

A different kind of music had taken over the bridge. Part of it could be traced to Arex, whose present navigational concerns were restricted to plucking and strumming the proper notes on an odd, double-stringed guitar. It wasn't an easy instrument to play, even for him, but without three hands it would have been all but impossible.

He was managing, however, singing a sweet wordless chant in time to the music. In the center of the floor, several of the younger officers were dancing lightly to the unusual rhythm, taking no notice of its alienness. And someone had broken out an adequate supply of intoxicants. It was developing into quite a party—even better, some insisted, than their recent private reveries on the Omicron pleasure world.

M'ress was leaning over the communications console while Scott, humming his own highland tune, massaged her shoulders. Her steady purring broke only once, when the chief accidentally rubbed her fur the wrong way. Otherwise, she was the picture of contentment.

Arex's wordless chant spiraled to a coda. It drew a smattering of applause from some of the listeners, who proceeded on to other activities.

Somewhere, in the back of the navigator's mind, a nonmusical note of insistence was howling for attention. Irritated, he glanced around the bridge, hoping something would key his memory. Oh yes, that was it.

"By the way," he murmured, speaking to the room

in general, "is anybody keeping a check on the captain and Mr. Spock?"

"Surre, Arrex, Surre," purred M'ress. "See?" She flicked a hand at a screen control indifferently, once, twice, hitting the activating switch on the third try. Scott took no notice of this highly arbitrary activity, continued to rub her shoulders and back. How soft the communications officer was! Scott did not seem concerned in the slightest that this was not an appropriate thought for a ship's chief engineer to have in regard to his back-up communications officer.

The small communications viewscreen lit up, but M'ress did not notice that. She was not bothering to look at it, seemingly having already forgotten why she turned it on. Arex didn't remind her. He'd good-naturedly responded to a request for another song. No one bothered to comment that the interference pattern which was all that showed on the screen, was not even in focus.

Neither was Arex's melody, but for some reason no one seemed to care about that, either. Mostly because the majority of the music was in their minds.

The solidifying transporter effect was more brilliant than usual under the cross-light of the twin suns as the two starship officers materialized within walking distance of the armored landing craft.

Extraordinarily, the usually exacting Chief Kyle had relaxed his control, because both men set down at a slant. Kirk adjusted quickly, righting himself. But Spock, in a gesture wholly out of character, did not. The first officer nearly fell over, and Kirk had to reach out to steady him. Spock looked back at the Captain and smiled warmly.

"Thanks, Jim. I've never done that before. It's good to have a friend like you." Kirk's expression started to twist up, but melted into an odd, warm smile.

"Strange, that's the way I feel about you, too. In fact

. . ." his smile grew broader, and he put a friendly arm around the first officer's shoulders ". . . my dear friend, Spock. Come on, let's go get Mudd and Christine." They started off down the slight slope in the direction of the lander. Neither man paid any attention to the slight shift in the surface of the ebony cliff behind them as the glistening medallion of the colossal eye opened again.

Mudd, preparing to unload some basic survival equipment for Chapel, had just stepped out of the lander onto the descending ramp. He did not even have a chance to notice the approaching officers before the ground began to shake.

Sand rattled around the base of the heavy vessel. The startled trader whirled. As he did so, Chapel shot past him before he could even think to get the phaser out or yell, or do anything else. She had spotted Kirk and Spock. But now she saw something else, and she screamed.

Ahead, black rock erupted from the earth, heaving skyward on six stumplike legs. Each was as big around as a starship warp-engine. Sand continued to drift down from little clefts and protuberances. Overall, the leviathan was faintly reptilian in appearance. However, this was just a human attempt to categorize, to make something utterly alien familiar. Actually, the beast resembled nothing that could be related to the fauna of Earth.

Its eye was wide open now, staring down at them with massive, blank malevolence.

Kirk and Spock heard Chapel scream, noticed her frantic gestures and turned. At the same time there was a loud sucking noise, and they saw the creature lift itself out of the sand. They ran to the lander.

There was no time for greetings, and they immediately ran from the craft as the monstrosity behind them swung around on pillarlike forelegs. Mudd, completely

stunned by the approaching apparition, was stumbling
around on the landing ramp.

A shadow crept over the lander as a three-taloned
cloud-paw blotted out the suns. The change in illumination was enough to shock Mudd into action. He ran
down the ramp and hurried to catch up with Chapel
and the others. Darkness fell just behind him as the
paw began to lower. It seemed to descend in slow motion. He heard a flat, ugly crunching sound as hundreds
of tons of living mountain ground the landing craft into
the sand. The paw, still moving with seemingly con-
trived slowness, slid under the pulverized metal.

The monster lifted the flattened lander up, up. It
looked like a broken toy in the shuttlecraft-sized paw.
One eye examined it cursorily, then the paw shook, and
the remnant of the lander flew free. It smashed down
near the terrified humans, and that action seemed to
galvanize the mountain-thing into motion once more.

Like a starship coming about, the monster turned,
revealing as it did not one but three eyes, spaced evenly
around the irregular, massive head. It had no recognizable neck—just the titan body and its six herculean
legs. A mouth opened, circular and irislike, to show a
bottomless pit lined with stalactites and stalagmites of
writhing, twisting cilia.

A shrill whistling sound echoed from that awesome
maw, like wind from a deep cave.

Spock, Kirk, and Chapel had slowed slightly, and
Mudd caught up to them. Hand shaking wildly, the
trader now raised his phaser toward the more threatening arrival. He tried to steady it by grabbing the wrist
with his free hand, but that only made the phaser shake
twice as hard.

Ignoring the ineffectual Mudd, Kirk and Spock
moved slightly apart, taking out their own weapons.

"Aim for the head!" Kirk instructed, more for
Mudd's benefit than for the calm Spock. Two beams of
red light shot upward, converged on the massive, eye-

studded bluff looming overhead. To Chapel they looked impossibly tiny, threadlike, to have much effect on that mountainous form. But if nothing else, the results proved conclusively that the creature was made of flesh and not unfeeling stone.

There was a tremendous whistling sound, a hurricanelike scream, and the beast exploded even further out of the sand. A long tentacular shape, something like a branching taproot, ripped out of the soil with an audible sucking noise. The creature snapped at itself where the beams had made contact, triple eyes blinking in dull pain.

Two of the gigantic legs collapsed, and the thing half fell to the ground, making the earth quake. The four humans were tossed about like corn in a popper.

The monster recovered as quickly as it had reacted, struggling back up onto all six legs. The great head, like the bow of a ship, turned ponderously, searching once again for its mote-sized tormentors. It had almost located the four bipedal specks sprawled helplessly on the dark sand when there was a rumbling from nearby, like distant thunder.

Suddenly the triorbed skull swung back in the opposite direction. A volcanic upheaval of sand was in progress behind it. Another black head appeared from the earth, followed by an equally gargantuan form, as a second monster lifted toward the blue-white sun. Once clear, it immediately started for the other.

The four spectators were alternately fascinated and fearful. Spock was the first to break free of the hypnotic thrall the incipient conflict had created. He grabbed the hypnotized Christine. That action shocked her as much as the dual appearance of the mountain-sized aliens. But still greater surprises were to come.

"Darling!" Spock gasped, "are you all right?"

"I'm fine, Mr. Spo—" She suddenly felt faint. "D . . . darling?

Mudd's expression was more easily interpreted. "Kirk, get us out of this!"

"Calm down, Harry," Kirk answered with an assurance he didn't feel. He freed his communicator, shook some clinging sand free, and flipped it open. As long as the monsters were occupied with one another, the humans were in no danger despite their proximity to them. A few seconds and they would be back on the ship.

"Transporter room—Captain speaking. Beam us up, Kyle, and show some speed."

On board the *Enterprise*, his voice sounded clearly over the open transporter room pickup. But it was lost in the music pouring gaily through the intership intercom.

Transporter Chief Kyle and an attractive young yeoman named Marion were dancing to the music. Kyle heard, or thought he heard, Kirk's voice, punctuated by the insistent clamor of the intercom alarm buzzer. But the strident sound blended easily, naturally, into the music.

Kyle held Yeoman Marion a little closer, smiling down at her. There was country fiddling and a Bruch concerto mixed somehow into the music—and something more. She returned his smile lovingly.

"No response," Kirk muttered, a little worriedly. The communicators were tough little instruments, wellsealed. It was virtually impossible for anything like sand to get inside. Kirk shook it, an age-old gesture of semimagic, and tried again.

"Chief Kyle, this is an emergency! Beam up!"

Not a hum of recognition in answer, nothing to show that the *Enterprise* still existed in this universe.

"What's going on up there!" Then he noticed that no one down here was paying him much attention, either.

Chapel appeared to have regained control of herself—and lost it in the process. The contradiction was implied, but not real. She was clinging to Spock and gazing up at him with a thoroughly unprofessional expression.

Mudd was pointing in the direction of the ruined landing craft and making indecipherable gobbling sounds. He was communicating, nonetheless.

After eyeing each other uncertainly for several long moments, the two moving mountains had turned slowly until both were once again facing the tiny aliens.

"Don't be upset with Chief Kyle, Jim," said Spock airily. "It takes a moment or two to lock in coordinates. It doesn't matter." He looked down at Chapel reassuringly. "Nothing matters, now that you're safe, Christine."

"Yes—oh yes. How wonderful."

"They're coming for us again!" Mudd stammered, backing up and making shoving gestures in the direction of the black monsters—gestures that were instinctive more than anything else.

The two giants were indeed moving toward them again, one ponderous step at a time. Kirk searched the landscape around them desperately. A thick cluster of towering yellow-brown knife-blades—the still standing core of some long-dead, long-eroded volcano—thrust out of the sand not too far behind them.

The weathered rock—if indeed it was rock, and not another monster—had been shattered in the past by some powerful convulsion that slivered it with deep cracks and crevices. There seemed to be a number of places to hide in. Anything was better than standing on the flat sand, waiting for a mountainous paw to flatten them.

"Over there!" Kirk yelled, starting toward the volcanic plug. Spock helped Chapel along while Mudd brought up the rear.

They made rapid progress over the sand, which fortunately grew firmer the nearer they came. And their approach provoked no display of eyes, legs, mouth, or

any other organic appurtenances. Kirk continued to rail
at the silent communicator.

"Emergency beam up—*Enterprise*, come in!" He
looked back over a shoulder. The first thing he saw was
that Spock and Chapel were running while tightly
locked together. Absurdity combined with apprehension to spark bitter comment.

"Can't you take your hands off her, even now?"

"This is my affair, Captain," Spock panted,
maintaining his dignity.

Chapel listened to this interplay without really understanding what was happening, or why. "Please, I
think we should get a few things straight . . ."

But she found it hard to talk while running. They
hurried into a deep crevice filled with sand, stumbling
back down arrow-straight depths that showed no signs
of narrowing. They had been lucky—their first choice
of a refuge was good and deep.

"Jim," Spock began, and then a switch was thrown
in his mind and he paused in confusion. "No . . . no
. . . Captain." He pronounced the title carefully,—em-
phasizing it—but then half-smiled again.

"We're both reacting abnormally. Look at me. It's
the potion. The love drug . . . insidious. It—" From behind them a loud voice interrupted incredulously.

"The love potion . . . insidious?" Mudd gaped at
them. Kirk and Spock ignored the trader.

Spock was fighting with himself. "Once . . . once you
recognize its effects for what they are, you're able to
resist it somewhat, as I am doing now."

"It worked," Mudd mumbled inanely, his facial expression one of dazed comprehension. "Oh my Great
Aunt Anabella, bless her departed black-hearted soul,
it worked!" He slumped dejectedly to the sand.

"And I was going to sell the few crystals I had left to
those lump-headed miners for a miserable three hundred credits apiece." Both hands beat at the sides of his
head.

"You mean you thought all along they were phony?" a puzzled Kirk asked, his attention momentarily drawn away from the communicator.

Mudd looked across at him, his voice a pitying moan. "Did you think I'd believe a crazy old Sirius medicine man? Of course I thought they were phony. Especially after all they did on Ilyria was make people sick." He was wallowing in self-misery.

"Old and crazy—wouldn't even say where the benighted things came from. I knew they could produce a temporary pleasant effect, and a little dizziness—but love?" He beseeched the heavens. "It's not fair, I tell you, it's not fair!"

The con-man conned—Kirk had to grin. He peered down the cleft. Neither of the creatures was in view. They had not seemed particularly intelligent, and their reaction time was slow, very slow. If only they didn't accidentally pass this way. Perhaps it would seem to them that the fast-moving tiny animals—themselves— had simply disappeared. If their memories were commensurate with their reactions, the two living mountains might go back to being pieces of scenery again.

"Cheer up, Harry. You wouldn't have known what to do with any honest money anyway." Mudd was too depressed to offer a rejoinder. He felt sick.

Perhaps the scene in the *Enterprise*'s Sick Bay might have cheered him up. Light music played over the intercom. Some of the medical personnel present were dancing close together. Others were playing idly with the medical computers.

A couple of the more adventurous were doing nonregulation things with the body-function machinery that slid over the hospital tables.

The nominal head of this sybaritic setting was Dr. McCoy. At the moment he had one arm companionably around Nurse Mayer.

"Now Lyra, did I ever tell you about the time I

saved Captain Kirk's life? And Commander Spock's?"
Nurse Mayer shook her head, looking up at him with a
mixture of awed admiration and affection. Her normal
reaction to such a statement of McCoy's would have
been a hard-boiled snort of derision.

"And my dear friend Scotty, too," McCoy continued
blithely. "And that pretty little Lieutenant Uhura.
Why, I guess I've saved just about everybody on this
ship, one time or another." He looked around the
room, saw nothing unusual in the highly unmedical activity.

"If the *Enterprise* had a heart, I'd save her, too." He
found himself sniffing away a tear, smiled down at her
his companion. "Let's talk about your heart, my dear
Lyra—"

Kirk walked over to Mudd, backed the trader up
against one wall. "How long does the effect of the potion last, Harry?"

"I . . . I don't know." Kirk reflected that he was still
probably in shock. Not from the sudden appearance of
the monsters, but from the revelation that he had probably been involved in an honest deal. "I didn't know it
was going to have any lasting effects at all, so I didn't
ask."

"Well how long," pressed an exasperated Kirk, "did
the 'crazy old medicine man' say it was *supposed* to
last?"

"Not long."

"What do you mean, 'not long'? He must have told
you something about its effects—whether you thought
they were foolish or not."

"Actually—you're hurting my arm, Captain—he was
starting to, but I wanted to complete the transaction as
smoothly as possible before he discovered the credit
slips I paid him with were counterfeit."

"Then how—" but Kirk was interrupted by a startled

shout from Chapel. He turned from Mudd, saw her pointing toward the entrance of the cleft.

Both monsters lumbered into view, blocking out much of the light as they moved between the setting suns and the crevice. Their heads, black icebergs, swayed slowly from side to side in searching motions. Then they stopped. The head of the nearest one stared into the cleft, three great glassy eyes pinning the humans under an overpowering, unthinking gaze.

Kirk handed his communicator to Chapel. "Keep trying to contact the *Enterprise*, Nurse." He looked from Mudd to Spock.

"Maybe we can divert them, somehow."

"That is an outstandingly stupid idea, Captain," Spock commented. He stopped, flustered. "I'm sorry, Captain, it's the drug. I simply doubt that we can successfully appeal to their better nature—if they have one. Nor do I think they would respond to having their backs scratched—it would take a landing craft to make an impression. And phaser fire only seems to make them madder."

"I wasn't thinking of anything like that, Spock. There's a terran expression that dates from ancient times, 'make love, not war.' Harry, do you have any of those crystals left?"

"Check his shoes, Captain. They're like his head," Chapel suggested. But it wasn't necessary. Mudd was voluntarily going through his pockets—and he found something. One hand came out, started to open, and then clamped tight. He started to slide away, along the wall.

"No, they're worth a fortune. My friends, dear Christine—" He was appealing to all of them. "I'll share it with you, I'll—"

Kirk reached out easily and clamped a hand around Mudd's wrist, smiling tightly.

"Ah, Captain, you're hurting me again. This archaic

resort to crude physical force isn't like you, Captain."
Mudd was trying very hard to keep smiling.

"Another second, Harry, and I'll crudely break it.
Don't worry. When you're unconscious, you don't feel
any pain."

"Since you put it that way, Captain—" His palm
opened reluctantly, and Kirk took the three crystals
thus revealed. Mudd bit his lower lip as he watched
them go. "Perhaps just one, Captain? To encourage my
continuing an honest career?"

But Kirk was already moving toward the entrance of
the now blocked crevice.

IX

On the bridge, the air was empty of all music. Not having effected actual contact with the love potion, but only inhaled a diluted vapor from it, the rest of the crew was rapidly reverting to normal.

M'ress started to stretch, stopped, and snarled. One paw went to her head, and she rubbed it tiredly. It seemed she'd been at some kind of party.

Scott walked over to her, exhibiting similar signs of an inner pain. "I've got a hangover to rank with the finest," he mumbled loudly. His voice rose to a near shout as he further declared, "And I dinna touch a dram o' that scotch!"

"Not so loud, you idiot!" M'ress pleaded, now putting both hands to her ringing head.

"Idiot, is it? Well, all of a sudden I'm not so crazy about you, either, Lieutenant." Scott glared at her.

The ground-to-ship channel crackled for attention. "Surface party to *Enterprise*—surface to *Enterprise*," came a weary voice barely recognizable as belonging to Head Nurse Christine Chapel. "Emergency beam up . . . repeat, request emergency beam up."

Both officers reacted simultaneously, looking at each other in surprise.

M'ress broke free of it, slapped over a switch, and snarled into the mike. "*Enterprise* here . . . is that you, Nurse Chapel? What's going on?"

Chapel nearly stumbled in her excitement. "Captain, I made contact!"

"Marvelous," a grim-faced Kirk replied, from up ahead. "I hope we last long enough to be beamed up."

The first leviathan was nearing the cleft. Any moment now a massive paw might rise up, descend on the rim of their refuge. The rock overhead seemed strong enough to keep even that heavy blow from them, but they were sure to be buried under an avalanche of loosened stone.

"It's seen me," Kirk yelled back to the others, hugging to the side of the cleft. "I need something to draw its attention. Phasers, Spock."

Spock moved to stand in the open, and a trembling Mudd forced himself to follow.

Holding the crystals in his right hand, phaser ready in his left, Kirk dashed out of the crevice.

He ran directly toward the first creature. Eyes the size of shuttle-bay doors inclined slowly to follow him.

Kirk ran to his right now, staying close against the base of the plug. As soon as the great head had turned to the side to follow him, Spock and Mudd fired.

Once again two beams of concentrated energy made contact with the skull. Once more the monster bucked, shrieking. The cavernous mouth opened.

Running down from the shielding stone and toward the living mountain, Kirk arched his arm, throwing the crystals with all his strength. They flew up and disappeared somewhere down that endless dark tunnel.

The mouth shut tight. The head swung back down toward Kirk and stopped. He watched it, paralyzed by those pondlike eyes. It hadn't made anything as recognizable as a swallowing motion—but then they had no idea what the monster's digestive system was like. In any case, there was no point in hesitating. All bets were placed; it was time to declare their hand.

Kirk ran toward the nearest enormous limb and slapped it firmly with both hands, twice. If this failed to work he was likely to die any minute. At least it might give Spock, Chapel, and Mudd a chance to beam up.

"Kyle!" M'ress was shouting into the intership communicator, "Transporter Chief Kyle, acknowledge!"

In the transporter room, Kyle searched frantically for the suddenly elusive intercom controls, finally located them. "Kyle here ... I think. What's wrong, Lieutenant?"

"Are you utterly incompetent?" M'ress howled, ignoring her own recent lapse in efficiency. "Didn't you hear—the Captain's requesting emergency beam up!"

"Emergency—I've been," a hand went to his forehead. "I've been ill."

"We've all been ill. For Amara's sake, Chief, beam them up!"

"Yes ... yes," groaned Kyle, his head ringing with M'ress's command. "I'll do anything ... only please stop shouting." He broke off and began working frantically at the transporter controls.

Kirk stumbled backward. The massive leg he had just touched was lifting skyward, seemingly propelled by a hidden crane. It hung poised there for a moment, then started to descend. He looked in all directions, but there was no place to run, and he was too far out to get back to the cleft.

The cliffside near him now was a solid wall, without even a cubbyhole to squirm into. The paw came down slowly, slowly. He closed his eyes and waited for death.

There was a deep, muffled thump—then nothing. He blinked.

The nearest talon, one of three massive hooks sprouting from the paw, had slammed down just next to him. It moved sideways, knocking him on his back gently.

Kirk looked upward, above the claw, to the looming face. It stared down at him blankly, expressionless and alien. Rolling over carefully, he caught his breath and then threw a handful of sand into the air, letting out a joyful whoop.

Spock, Mudd, and Chapel had moved to the edge of

the crevice to watch the drama play itself out. They started to cheer, and Kirk ran jubilantly to join them.

"It worked, by God, it worked!" Mudd seemed to be sniffling and mumbling something about his lost riches, but the others were sharing Kirk's excitement.

They were stunned to silence by a screaming whistle.

They had forgotten about the second monster.

Cilia fluttering around the inside of its mouth, the other monster had turned toward the cleft entrance and was heading for them. Kirk scrambled backward with the others, drawing his phaser. Spock and Mudd lifted theirs a moment later.

Another whistling shriek shattered the dry air. The second beast halted its ponderous attack as a gigantic paw swung past barely missing it. The first monster had spun around and now blocked the path of the second.

The wave of sand thrown up by the first creature inundated Kirk and the others, knocking them off their feet and burying Spock up to his waist. Mudd lost his phaser and Kirk his. They scrambled to free themselves.

A reverberating tremor followed as the two beast-mountains slammed into each other, multiple legs clawing at sides and face, circular mouths straining for a vacuuming grip on uneven body surfaces.

Kirk nearly fell again as they retreated back into the cleft. A rear leg swung wildly and tore away meters of cliff-face near the top of the crevice. A shower of rock came down, barricading the humans inside the cleft.

The earth shook as the two titans threw blow after blow at one another. Every time one of the multiple-ton paws connected, there was a clap like thunder.

The second beast struck a powerful blow, knocking the first aside, and was battered off its feet in turn. As it tumbled, the gigantic skull crashed against the front of the sheltering cleft and jammed there, cracking free more rock. A monstrous evil eye glared directly at them.

One huge front leg shoved the creature to its feet again. The other lifted and reached inward, straining for the four trapped figures, descending toward four sparkling pillars of rainbow-hued light, finally landing to scoop out a deep pit in the sand where Kirk, Spock, Mudd, and Chapel had stood helplessly only seconds before.

"And then, on Ophiucus VI," Mudd continued, his cheerful form wavering from behind the vision-distorting force-field, "I conned two miners out of a year's supply of dilithium crystals with fake Federation credit vouchers." He grinned in remembrance.

"They weren't too hysterical about that, though, miners are very philosophical types. We might have settled the misunderstanding amicably, if only they hadn't discovered so soon that the Andalusian pleasure slave I'd given them in exchange for the fake vouchers was a pneumatic automaton. That's when they became rather nonplussed—though that wasn't the exact term they used—and I was forced to bid a hasty adieu to their charming frontier world."

"May I be of help in recording the confession, Nurse Chapel?" Spock inquired helpfully. He had just exited from the elevator, curious to find out how the recording was going. Chapel put a temporary hold on the recorder and looked up at him bitterly.

"You? You'd be the last person I'd choose." Her gaze traveled from the first officer's foot to his head, then turned sharply away Spock merely raised his eyebrows, then turned his attention over to Mudd.

"A few minutes of love, now to be paid for with many hours of hatred—the usual way of human emotions, it seems. I do not think your potion would be a very good buy even at half the price, Harry Mudd."

"Ah well, Spock, you know how it is," Mudd replied easily. "So few things in this universe live up to their reputations."

"Except you, Harry. I should say that you live up to yours in a style few other sentients can boast of—or would want to."

"As neat a backhanded compliment as ever I've had, Spock," Mudd appplauded. His head cocked questioningly to one side. "Think I'll get rehabilitation therapy again?"

"I would almost guarantee it, Harry Mudd, though I fail to observe any beneficial effects in you of such past treatment."

"No, it doesn't seem to work too well on me, does it?" Mudd agreed. "It's not easy, you know, Spock, when you're born with a name like Mudd. At least I do have, as you say, the virtue of consistency."

"In your case, Harry, it's hardly a virtue."

"Rehabilitation therapy," murmured Chapel, her eyes gleaming. One hand opened and closed rhythmically. She stared through the force-field.

"I think maybe it would do Harry more good if he had a dose of good old-fashioned cruel and unusual punishment instead."

"Now, now, my dear Christine," Mudd said, "is that a proper attitude for a dispenser of healing to have? Besides, I'm an official Federation prisoner, and as such I'm entitled to a little—"

"Maybe you'd better finish this for me, after all, Mr. Spock," she said, staring at Mudd with a look Florence Nightingale would have found appalling. She handed him the tricorder, clenching both hands nervously behind her back.

"I should think you would be getting used to rehabilitation therapy by now," Spock mused conversationally, his scientific curiosity aroused.

"You never get used to it, Spock, but that doesn't matter. That's not what's really bothering me."

"There is something troubling you more than the prospect of renewed therapy?" Spock noted. "Most interesting."

"You see," Mudd continued, "it's only that I hate to leave you all." He smiled dangerously. "All my loved ones . . ."

Despite the fact that Mudd was declared absolutely off limits to all members of the crew, that his meals were always served up by automatons, and that no one visited him for whatever reason except in twos, Kirk didn't relax until they had entered orbit around Starfleet sector headquarters at Darius.

They gave him back his own clothes, then—minus the astonishing assortment of miniature devices concealed within the material—turned him over to an escort party made up of Kirk's best security people.

Cheerful to the last, Mudd waved friendly good-byes to them all as he was turned over to ground-based Peaceforcer personnel. He was still waving as they led him through the sliding doors of the Legal Building.

Watching him depart, Kirk couldn't help but wonder if Mudd were not already at work trying to convince his escorts into not only letting him go, but into turning over their identification cards and weapons as well.

If he got a single ranking official into a card game, the planet was lost.

Kirk hoped for at least a moderate layover. But as it developed there was no time to rest and enjoy the pleasures Darius had to offer. Orders were waiting for him as soon as he and the security party beamed back aboard.

"'Communication from Starfleet Science Headquarters, Captain," said Sulu as Kirk reentered the bridge. "Confidential. Mr. Spock is waiting for you in your quarters."

"Thank you, Mr. Sulu."

Well, that was fast. Something especially interesting must be up if Spock felt the need of discussing the orders in private.

The first officer of the *Enterprise* was seated at the

large central desk in Kirk's rooms. He swiveled to face the Captain as he entered.

"I trust, Captain, that Harry Mudd is safe in custody?"

"I'd feel better if they would give his tongue rehabilitation therapy instead of his mind. One appears to operate independently of the other. But I think we've seen the last of Harcourt Fenton Mudd—I hope."

"I understand from Mr. Sulu that you've kept the new orders secret. By their urgency I gather that they don't alllow us time for a rest orbit."

"It would appear not, Captain, though I have only played the first portion of them." He hefted a small microtape cassette. "Here is the communication from Science Center. I think you will find it interesting." He slipped the cassette into the desk play-back slot. Kirk sat down.

A young science officer appeared on the screen in front of them. He was standing alone in a chamber that gave signs of extending above and behind him to considerable distances. The camera pulled back and showed that this was indeed the case. It also identified the particular chamber to Kirk and Spock.

Rising from floor almost to ceiling was a full-scale reproduction of the Megasphere—the gigantic artificial construct which was an exact model of the Milky Way. Distances between the stars, nebulae, black holes, neutron stars, and other objects were to scale—though the stars and other intragalactic objects were not. If so represented, they would have had to have been built so small as to be visible only under a microscope.

All galactic coordinates for starship navigational computers and all scientific referents to galactic structure were drawn from the Megasphere. Only two originals existed—one on Earth, the other on Vulcan.

New stellar discoveries were constantly being added, a titanic task in itself, as the proper insertion of a newly charted star into the Megasphere was work for specially designed computer controlled microhandlers. As it was, maintaining accuracy within the colossal model was a job involving weeks of preparation merely to design new microhandlers to perform the actual insertion.

Banks of special lights flooded the Megasphere from every angle. The light was picked up, amplified, and thrown back into near darkness by special photosensitive material. Bulbs or any kind of powered light source were too clumsy and too difficult to use. The photosensitive material used would never wear out, never need replacement.

Half a dozen special gravity field generators held the stellar model intact, any one of which could maintain the Megasphere. If for some unforseeable reason all six failed simultaneously, the work of years would fall to the chamber floor in a shower of tiny glowing pebbles.

The young officer spoke easily, with the manner of a confident lecturer.

"Captain Kirk, Science Officer Spock . . . I am Lieutenant Bell of the Prometheus Science Center. I think you will be pleased to know that the new mission that you have been selected to carry out is of a purely investigative and scientific nature, with no rescue or Peaceforcer functions involved." He smiled pleasantly, and Kirk found himself liking this young man. That, he reminded himself, was exactly why Lieutenant Bell had been chosen to deliver recorded orders.

"But this assignment will require considerable long-range cruising, so we are concerned that you be on your way as soon as possible." Bell had a thin, glowing metal wand with which he turned and pointed into the Megasphere.

"Your approximate route . . ."

PART III

THE MAGICKS
OF MEGAS-TU

(Adapted from a script by Larry Brody)

X

Kirk really did not have the words for it. At times he had wished he'd been born with a little more of the poet in him. But after days and days of travel in which they had seen their objective grow progressively nearer, Kirk, like everyone else on board, had long since run out of superlatives. Now he was reduced to trying to relate the panorama in simple human terms.

The best description he could come up with was that it was like a soup of infinite ingredients and color. A sunsoup, a stellar gumbo.

Oh, they were all there—superhot blue-whites, blue giants, red dwarfs, supergiants, plain whites, cepheids, and irregular variables, binary and triple stars, with the younger stars predominating.

And a fair sampling of the familiar Sol-type, innocuous yet heart-breakingly familiar amid the splendor of iridescent gases and cosmic debris of all types and descriptions. No, soup seemed a thoroughly inadequate label for the center of the galaxy—but at least it didn't overwhelm. He found himself squinting as he studied the awesome panorama glowing on the main viewscreen.

"Turn down the brightness, Mr. Sulu." The cluster of cosmic matter was so dense now that the cumulative brightness on the screen hurt the eyes.

"It's down all the way, sir."

"Well then, put another filter over the scope."

"Aye, sir." Sulu touched a switch. Immediately the full brilliance of the tightly packed suns, gasses, and nebulae dimmed to a bearable level.

Kirk shook his head and envied a certain section of the *Enterprise*'s crew. It was an astronomer's paradise, and in fact that section of the ship's scientific complement was working round the clock by its own choice.

Kirk, of course, was too occupied with administrative details to enjoy more than this occasional quiet study of the starscape. He sighed, pressed a well-used button on the arm of the command chair.

"Captain's Log, stardate 5524.5. For many years scientists have theorized that the galazy was created by a great central explosion. If this was so, attendant new theories postulate that the galactic center may still be creating new matter.

"The *Enterprise* has the honor of being the first ship to attempt to penetrate to the heart of the galaxy. We will try to ascertain the truth or falsity of this and numerous other spatial hypotheses."

Despite the additional filter on the pickup telescope itself, the stunning brightness of the surrounding space continued to intensify. Gaseous and radioactive particle matter was so thick here that at times the *Enterprise* seemed to be drifting through a phosphorescent fog, a pale white submersible in a ocean of deep-sea fish. Readings on radiation meters remained within tolerable levels, but an older starship than the *Enterprise* would soon have had her crew fatally burned.

"Heading now zero zero one degrees due east of the galactic plane, Captain," Sulu broke in. "Maintaining indicated observation-recording speed of warp-one."

They were getting very close. A hand touched the button again. He would finish the log entry later.

"Maintain speed, Mr. Sulu. Correct ship to a heading of zero degrees." No other starship captain in history had been able to utter that momentous phrase, and it might be some time before another repeated it.

"The center of the galaxy," he murmured, for the umpteenth time. He looked over to the library computer station, where Spock, like the astronomers, had been working overtime just to record new information.

"I'm not sure what I'll do or how I'll react, if we find there actually is a central something that all matter springs from, like a well. How about you, Spock? Surely you've thought about it."

"From an astrophysical standpoint I find it all quite fascinating, Captain. Personally, I am more intrigued by what we may encounter there in the nature of subsidiary phenomena. How does gravity react at the center, for example.

"Yet I am afraid we shall be somewhat disappointed and find that the precise center is very much like the area immediately around it, an area such as we are traversing at this very moment," the science officer concluded.

"Galactic center in three minutes, Captain," Sulu reported.

"Thank you, Mr. Sulu. Lieutenant Uhura, sound yellow alert, as planned."

"Aye, sir, yellow alert." Uhura proceeded to make the necessary demands on her instrumentation. The proper alarm signal pealed out.

There was a short wait, then the communications officer looked back at him. "All decks and stations report yellow-alert status effected, Captain."

"Ready for whatever comes, then," Kirk whispered to himself, and added aloud, "I hope."

"What was that, Captain?"

"Nothing, Mr. Spock. Nothing."

At first it seemed as if Spock's dry evaluation was going to turn out to be correct. Nothing unique appeared on the screen; they saw nothing not already previously encountered.

Then it appeared with unexpected suddeness. Somewhere directly ahead was a phenomenon different from anything any of the bridge complement had ever seen.

At first glance it resembled a small nebula trying to turn itself inside out. But it was no normal nebula according to the sensors. The writhing, twisting mass of color was in constant violent motion, spitting out particles and gasses in all directions.

"Mr. Spock," said Kirk quickly, but the science officer was already attending to his recorders.

"Visual contact galactic center, Captain," he reported. "The volume of energy and mass here is overwhelming. Instrumentation can only calibrate a portion of the total flux—their levels don't read any higher."

"All right, Spock, be careful. There's enough energy out there to overload every sensor on the ship." He need not have said it; he was only verbalizing what was obvious to Spock and everyone else.

Kirk stared at the screen, thoroughly mesmerized. There was no form, no pattern, no structure to that violent, churning whirlpool of force.

"Evaluation, Mr. Spock."

"It is indeed the theorized creation point, Captain. Detectors indicate it is putting forth a tremendous amount of particulate matter, from the subatomic levels mostly. There are also new, as yet unidentifiable, structures . . . Also radioactive gasses, free energy. Fortunately we do not have to make interspace calls from here—they would be drowned out a meter from the hull."

"Okay, Spock, we know what's coming out. Is anything going in?" That would be the critical test. Spock's answer would eventually make a number of astronomers happy.

"Very little, if anything, Captain. There are indications that the fabric of space in the immediate vicinity of the creation point is not stable."

"That's hardly surprising," Kirk observed, "in view of the forces at work here."

"Despite the evidence of considerable gravitation potential," Spock continued, as if he were talking about the most common household object, "there is no sign of hydrogen or anything else being drawn into the center from the surrounding space. Altogether an extraordinary phenomenon. I believe we may be looking at the rarest single structure in the known universe: a negative black hole—one that ejects, rather than attracts matter."

Kirk nodded. "That would confirm that all matter in our universe has been drawn from other universes, and that creation is truly infinite, as some theories state."

"Merely because our galaxy draws its substance from the black hole of another universe, Captain, and that our black holes may each well be the galactic center of other star clusters, does not mean that the universe itself is infinite—only somewhat larger than we had suspected."

Kirk wondered at his first officer. Only Spock could concede the possible existence of a billion billion other *universes* and make it come out as an understatement.

He returned his attention to the viewscreen, but it was only a moment before Spock glanced up from his hooded viewer again.

"There is also evidence of other forces at work here, Captain, which are unclassifiable under standard astronomical referents. I would strongly suggest that we—" He stopped.

An automatic stylus was beginning to jiggle up and down on the console to his left. As he watched it, the oscillation increased. Finally it became violent enough to knock the stylus loose from its holder. It rolled off the slanted console onto the deck.

At the same time Spock grabbed at the console edges. The *Enterprise* had begun a rocking motion, sideways, then up and down, then sideways again.

"Easy," said Kirk to everyone in general and no one in particular.

The buffeting grew more violent. "Reverse power, hold this position, then head zero zero one degrees left." They would use this strange new force to help slip around the storm of the center itself. "Deflector screens on full."

"Deflectors up, sir," Sulu informed him, adding, "it's taking considerable power to maintain this heading, sir."

"We'll hold it, Mr. Sulu," said Kirk calmly.

The buffeting didn't vanish entirely, but the increased power being fed to the warp-engines seemed sufficient to reduce it to an occasional sharp tremor. No one was in danger of being thrown from his seat.

The *Enterprise* continued to move around the fiery core.

"Good heavens—look at that!" Sulu exclaimed. Kirk's attention had not varied from the screen, but he understood Sulu's automatic shout. "Just a moment, sir . . . I'll widen the angle." The helmsman worked controls.

Abruptly their field of vision seemed to quadruple, and the phenomenon revealed by their new position became fully visible.

Once again, superlatives were insufficient.

Lines of pure force had grown so strong they had begun to radiate. They stretched from the spastic central core out to the nearest suns in great flaring arcs. Everyone on the bridge, who thought he was past amazement, sat enthralled by the spectacle. The lines glowed and shifted slightly and were to a solar prominence what a spider's web would be to a suspension bridge.

"I wonder," Kirk murmured, "if the surrounding stars hold the creation point steady, via these lines of force, at the center of our galaxy?" Or was the creation point fighting a constant battle, through millions and millions of less detectable lines of force, to hold its myriad suns around it?

"Charting scanners on, Captain," Spock said smoothly. "Commencing official survey central quadrant." Less sophisticated instruments took over now, as formal mapping was begun.

The doors to the bridge elevator slid aside, and McCoy entered, moving quickly.

"Jim, Spock—" Another jolt rocked the bridge. "What in the name of sanity is going . . . ?" His voice trailed off. He had just gotten his first glimpse of the mind-boggling panorama spread across the screen.

"What on Earth is that?"

"Nothing we can detect from Earth itself, Bones—or even from nearby. We're here—at the center of the galaxy—and all the theories and guesses and hypotheses about this place appear to have been right . . . with frosting."

They all watched as the *Enterprise* continued to move past the central core.

For the first time, an uncertain tone seemed to be present in Spock's voice. "Captain, we appear to be moving up on a completely new phenomenon."

"Another one?"

Apparently they were not out miracled yet. Something different was indeed showing up on the viewscreen.

Kirk saw that some of the feathery lines of iridescent force, instead of leaping out toward nearby stars in smooth arcs, had twisted together. They were curling and writhing violently about themselves, a concatenation of energy separate from the core being manipulated by a galactic potter's wheel.

The forces created by this secondary center took on a definite shape as they moved closer. Instead of the central chaos, they formed a recognizable, colossal cone. It was visible only when destroyed matter at its edges exploded, or when a force-line flared with a discharge of energy that would dwarf the output of several suns.

Yet sensors revealed that instead of putting out energy-matter like the center point, here it was being drawn inward. But it was most definitely not a black hole, nor a neutron star. It was something as new as the negative black hole of Spock's hypothesis, and something even less recognizable.

A number of stars swirled like dust motes about its rim, spinning crazily. Occasionally one would impinge on the edge of the cone itself. The result was a flare of light—overwhelming if compared to a human-generated explosion, yet far from nova-sized.

Sulu shattered the awed contemplation. "Captain, I'm up to warp-six for flyby on revised course, but that thing seems to be pulling us in. Yet the gravity detectors show no new change in the surrounding field. I don't understand the forces operating here. And it's not a computer malfunction, sir. Our course is definitely being affected."

Even as he spoke, strong vibration rocked the bridge. Yet it was somehow different from before.

"Scanners indicate the energy cone is composed of both matter and energy, like the core itself." Spock said, checking his readouts. "But there appears to be some kind of order at work here, whereas the core point was anarchical in nature.

"There is indeed some powerful attractive force operating within the vortex, but it is, as Mr. Sulu has stated, something other than normal gravity. Something outside our experience, I fear."

"Warp-seven, Captain," the excited Sulu interrupted. "Warp-eight!"

"Take us out of here, Mr. Sulu," Kirk ordered; but the helmsman was already working at his console.

"I've been trying to, sir. We're still being drawn in. Warp-nine . . . warp-ten, sir!"

"Emergency reverse power!"

Back at his post in engineering central, Scott noticed the sudden terrific demands being made on his engines. He held tight to a crossbar to keep from being thrown to the floor by the increasingly wild vibrations and hoped the drive could cope with the forces being pitted against them.

As the *Enterprise* was drawn inexorably nearer the energy vortex, the colors on the viewscreen began to pulse violently, the pastel rainbow giving way to deep golds and reds, all being subsumed into a vital, rippling purple.

Now the ship had been pulled to the very rim of the cosmic cyclone. It hung there a second, then caught and started to spin at tremendous speed around the rim, faster, and faster. On the *Enterprise* the artificial gravity compensators could barely keep up with the steady increase in centrifugal force.

Scott now clung desperately to the crossbar and stared grim-faced at his gauges. Shouts of pain and groans came from various members of his staff who had failed to gain a firm purchase on something immovable.

Somehow, hanging tight with both legs and one arm against the terrific sideways pressure, he managed to pull himself a hand at a time to the nearest wall intercom. From there he tried to raise the bridge.

"Captain . . . Scott here. I don't know how much additional emergency power we can continue to put out before the engines start to break up."

Kirk listened but was helpless to acknowledge. He had been thrown to the floor. Despite the gravity compensators, the whirling was generating G-forces too powerful to be canceled out.

Spock was still seated in his chair at the library station, clinging tightly to the arms. He tried to shift for a still firmer grip. He felt a wrenching pull as the *Enterprise* hit an eddy in the rim of the vortex and was jerked loose. He slid past Kirk and came to a halt up against a console on the opposite side of the bridge.

"Spock . . . you all right?"

His reply ignored Kirk's query. "Captain, there may be only one choice open to us. We must hope this vor-

tex is analogous in its internal structure to Terran/Vul-
can counterparts ... hope that there is a calm in its
center where these forces either do not exist or cancel
each other out."

"Agreed, Mr. Spock. We'll try to make for the eye of
the cyclone—if it has one. Mr. Sulu, Mr. Arex ..."

But neither helmsman was in a position to carry out
orders. Sulu was jammed in a tangle of arms and legs
against Kirk's command chair, while Arex had skidded
all the way back to communications, despite the frantic
use of all six arms and legs. He lay pinned against
Uhura's feet.

Kirk gritted his teeth and struggled to pull himself
toward the deserted navigation console. As he moved,
he rose slightly off the deck and was bounced end over
end, coming to a stop against the library station.

"Allow me, Captain," said Spock. Now the G-forces
seemed to increase, decrease, and change direction
capriciously, making it far harder to judge one's movements. Up, down, and sideways changed without warning.

Uhura screamed as she was suddenly thrown and
pinned against the ceiling. Much more of this, Kirk reflected, and it wouldn't matter whether the ship broke
up or not, because her crew would long since have pre-
ceded her.

Somehow Spock managed to inch his way toward the
helm. There was a crackling discharge, and the deck
lights flashed on and off. More cracklings followed,
mixed with the groans of metal alloy strained to its utmost. Kirk revised his estimates of the approaching catastrophe.

The *Enterprise* would disintegrate first after all. They
would all experience the unique sensation of floating
free in the maelstrom before the surrounding radiation
and hard space would reduce them to their component
atoms.

Spock reached the helm. Bracing himself firmly with

one arm, he used the other to fumble at several controls. The *Enterprise* began to break away from the spinning, violent iridescence and move toward the center of the vortex.

It hung there motionless for several long seconds, warp-engines fighting to drive her outward and back into normal space. Then the ship began to drift, slowly at first but with steadily increasing speed, down the rapidly narrowing funnel.

But that was all. The vibrating ceased; the smell of overloaded circuits and the sound of tortured metal stopped, and the crushing centrifugal force was instantly wiped out. Once more they had a recognizable up and down, as the ship's artificial gravity computer finally restored some order.

Back in engineering, Scott had to duck as one of his technicians fell slowly past him. Kirk's voice sounded over the intercom.

"Engineering ... status report." By now Scott was on his feet again—though moving cautiously—and checking readouts. Several of the delicate instruments used to measure gravitation were completely gone, having been maltreated to the point of destruction. They no longer registered anything, since they had been overloaded even beyond emergency shutdown.

Scott whistled silently. Without the powerful gravity compensators, there would be nothing left of the crew of the *Enterprise* now but a multitude of brownish smears against floors, walls, and ceilings.

But the readings on the instruments that had survived intact were encouraging. Scott spoke toward the wide open pickup grid.

"There's some damage, Captain, but I think everything can be repaired." He groaned and reached for his lower back. "Includin' me."

"Okay, Scotty, do your best. We're running down the center of some kind of spiraling energy storm. I don't know how long we've got till we reach bottom, or what will happen when we get there. Be ready. Bridge out."

"Be ready, he says," Scott mumbled, "and for what?" Well, whatever it was, he would do his best to see that the *Enterprise* was ready for it.

"Gabler, Jacobs—there's nothin' wrong with you! Get off your duffs and break out a pair of microwelders. Some honest work's required of you, for a change!"

On the bridge, everyone was slowly rearranging himself, uncurling from various contorted positions. Fortunately, few of the sudden changes in gravity had been full-G, and the falls hadn't been as serious as they might have been. Arex gave Uhura, who had probably received the worse banging around, a hand up.

"Would you like to report to Sick Bay, Lieutenant?" asked Kirk worriedly.

"No, I'm all right, Captain," She eased herself slowly back into her seat, wincing. "I don't think the parts of me that hurt would benefit by lying down. They shouldn't impair my efficiency, either—and no remarks, Mr. Spock!"

Spock looked bewildered, and Kirk's smile deepened at his first officer's obvious confusion.

Spock finally decided to ignore what was evidently another touch of inexplicable human humor—preferring that to the thought that Uhura might be more seriously injured than she admitted.

"An incredible experience, Captain."

"Ah, it got to you emotionally, did it, Spock?" pressed McCoy.

"As usual, an incorrect interpretation of a straightforward observation, Doctor. I found it scientifically fascinating, of course."

"I don't suppose you were scared, either?"

"Scared, Doctor? I fail to see why one should be frightened of understandable natural phenomena. I do confess that for several moments, estimates of the forces acting unfavorably on the ship did not induce in me optimism as to our overall chances for survival, however—"

"Oh, never mind, Spock," McCoy turned his attention to Kirk. "At least I had the good sense to be scared, Jim. What now?"

Kirk stared up at the screen, which now showed a seemingly endless series of concentric circles of flaring violet light. The smallest circles tended to be dark to the point of blackness.

"Mr. Sulu?"

"We're moving down the vortex, as assumed, Captain," the helmsman reported, studying his instruments. "And at a speed nothing short of astronomical. The cone itself seemed nowhere near this long at first examination. Normal space–time laws are badly distorted here. The sensors appear to be functioning properly."

"Any chance of breaking free and making our way back to the rim?" Kirk asked. The helmsman's reply was sobering.

"We've been running at full reverse drive for several minutes, Captain."

"Um." Kirk digested this information quietly. "Stop the drive down to warp-two." There was no point in continuing useless demands on the engines—they might need all the power they could muster, later.

He turned back to McCoy, remembering the doctor's question. "We'll ride it through, Bones. What else can we do?"

"Ride it through to where?"

Spock replied with another of his overwhelming quiet pronouncements. "Perhaps to the center of All Things, Doctor."

McCoy was confused instead of awestruck. "But I thought we'd already passed by the center, Spock?"

"And so we did, Doctor. This vortex was completely unexpected. But to use both our worlds for a crude analogy—there is a fixed north pole on Earth and on Vulcan. Yet this is only a geographic convenience. There is also another 'north pole' that is the real center of natural forces."

"Magnetic north," added Kirk, "and it wanders around from year to year. I see your point, Spock. There may be two centers to the galaxy. A spatial one, from which all else can be measured—and another on which certain different forces converge."

"That is it, Captain," Spock admitted, "and it is that second convergence of forces that we appear to be traveling through to its end."

"Wherever that may be—and it looks like we'll be there soon." Kirk gestured, and all eyes returned to the main screen.

The violet light seemed to be blending, running together into a smooth maroon pool that glowed like a dim red giant. They struck it seconds later. But the *Enterprise* was moving so supremely fast by then that no matter what the malignant maroon eye was—red giant or otherwise—they were in and through it before any effect was noted.

A tremendous red flash did erupt around the ship. Crimson sparks and activated particles flew away from her hull, dissolving further into all the primary hues. At Spock's sensor station and the navigation consoles, every instrument went berserk.

There was a long silence.

"My, my," whispered McCoy, his the only voice on the bridge, as he and everyone else sat staring at the screen.

Space as they knew it was . . . gone.

In its place had been substituted the wild nightmare of a color-blind surrealist. Nothing seemed fixed or permanent. What at one moment appeared as the black of normal interstellar space, complete with distant stars, would suddenly fracture like a hemorrhaging amoeba into tiny patches of scattered darkness, still with stars, and turn unexpectedly magenta or maroon or red.

Now and then it appeared as if an ocean of white-hot magma was floating only a few hundred meters beneath the *Enterprise*. A moment later and it formed a glowing roof over their heads, then a wall to either side, continually throwing off bubbling blobs of itself which drifted off in all directions.

As the *Enterprise* moved through it, nonspace slowly started to coalesce, to take on a single form. It gradually became a kind of circular tunnel with unstable sides composed of a fluid yellow substance.

They existed in a yellow, cylindrical universe. As the *Enterprise* continued down the corridor the ship started to slow, its speed dropping from warp-impossible to warp-ten, to one and then sublight speed.

At first the flavescent corridor appeared to be at least a million meters in diameter. Now it had shrunk until the walls seemed ready to touch the hull itself. At the end of the corridor, rotating in its center and blocking further passage, was a spherical object that just might be a world.

"Is that a planet?" exclaimed Sulu, voicing the question in the mind of everyone. It was shockingly, paralyzingly stable-looking—the first truly stable-looking thing they had seen since entering the vortex.

Stable it might be, but normal it was not. It was striped in red and whites like a candy-cane Jupiter, though it was only slightly larger than Earth-size . . . if the sensors could be believed.

"What is it?" wondered Uhura aloud. "Where are we?"

Spock looked up from the hooded viewer at his station. "I am afraid that our normal navigational references mean very little here, Lieutenant. All readings indicate that we are not in time as we know it. That we are no longer in space as we know it has been self-evident for some time now" He looked at McCoy.

"Doctor, perhaps these readings may mean more to you," McCoy moved over and studied the information in the viewer.

Sulu had pushed away from the navigation console while Arex was idly running the fingers of three hands over various controls. He encountered switches and buttons with random nonchalance. It didn't matter what he hit, nothing produced the slightest reaction.

He looked back at Kirk. "The helm's dead, sir. Some of the instrumentation still registers information, but they don't make any sense. Most of the navigation readouts have simply fallen to zero."

Kirk make a noncommital noise, shifted his attention to communications. "Lieutenant Uhura, try to get a message through to Starfleet. They should at least know of our position here. Maybe someone can be reached at Science Center who has some helpful suggestions."

She worked at her machinery for several minutes, then glanced helplessly back over her shoulder.

"Captain, the subspace radio is dead, too. So are all pickups. I should at least be registering static from any energy flowing around us, but there's nothing, nothing at all."

At that point McCoy happened to notice the chronometer over Spock's station. He checked his own against it, then made a fast check with the still operating library computer.

"Jim, not only is there no time here as we *know* it, there doesn't seem to be any time. All the ship's chronometers have stopped. Emergency backup power doesn't seem to make any difference."

"Engineering to bridge."

"Bridge here, Captain speaking." By now Kirk was so numbed that Scott's announcement seemed inevitable instead of frightening.

"There's no reason for it, Captain, no reason at all," complained the stunned, puzzled voice of the chief engineer, "but the antimatter and matter generators are going ... fading out. Everything seems to be operating perfectly, the engines, converters, everything ... but they're just fading. We're losing power. Emergency storage cells are dropping rapidly, and I canna tell you why. Everythings coming ... to a ... stop." There was a sudden crackling, and they heard Scott's voice again, weaker now as the communicator power evaporated.

"... a ... top ..." There was a final fizzle and the intercom died for good.

As it did, the lights on the bridge went out. As with the intercom, the automatic emergency backups failed to take over.

"It would appear that none of the natural laws of our universe operate here, Captain," Spock observed. For once, even his tone was muted.

"Natural laws," McCoy echoed. "The life-support systems ... they're probably fading, too. Is everything just going to go ... out? Hey, I'm floating."

"So am I," came Kirk's voice from somewhere in the darkness nearby.

"And I," reported Sulu. One by one, the rest of them confirmed the loss of gravity.

Without light and gravity the universe lost all sense. There was no true direction, no sense of up or down— or of right and wrong. Kirk found himself curling into a fetal position as his mind tried vainly to cope with the absence of reality.

No! He forced himself to stick out his arms and legs. He would die in the shape of a man.

McCoy coughed, found himself propelled by the slight action. Eventually he bumped into something hard—whether floor or ceiling he could not tell. Then he noticed something else.

"Jim ... air's getting bad ... needs circulation ... cleaning."

Kirk tried to orient himself in the darkness as he spoke. It was hopeless. He could only pray that the open intercom would pick up his voice.

"Engineering!" he shouted, "we're getting stale air. Go to battery power on all circulation instrumentation. Primary alert, Scotty!"

Silence and soft darkness.

"Mr. Sulu."

"Here, Captain," came a reluctant, weak reply. The helmsman coughed slightly from somewhere nearby.

"Mr. Sulu," Kirk said slowly and distinctly, "there is an emergency. Go to battery power."

"I can't, Captain. I don't know where the console is."

"I am still holding my seat, Captain." Arex's voice! But Kirk's last hopes disappeared with the navigator's reply. "When the lights went I tried switching to reserves. There isn't any battery power on the bridge, either. Either they've been drained or they simply don't operate in this space-time continuum. I'm sure I tried the proper controls. Everything's gone dead." He coughed, and his voice faded to a thin wheeze.

". . . dead . . ."

"Arex?" Kirk inhaled and found himself choking. His hand went to his throat. Air . . . he was drowning, smothering, and the darkness was a blanket over him.

He heard a faint voice . . . McCoy. "Jim . . . Jim . . . we've got to do something . . . we've . . ." Then it, too, faded and was gone.

Gasping, Kirk tried to reach out to him, flailing in the emptiness, struggling to touch another human being a last time. He felt something, turned, straining. Another hand touched his and gripped tight.

"Captain?" Kirk couldn't see the figure next to him . . . yet in his mind he did.

"Good-bye, Mr. Spock."

"Good-bye, Captain . . ."

XI

Peace.

Night.

Blindness ... Kirk found himself blinded, dazzled, stunned by the unexpected flare that lit the bridge in scintillating geometric patterns. It fluoresced in the unnatural brilliance. The strange designs pulsed for a few seconds longer, then disappeared.

Kirk felt his vision returning as his outraged retinas began to cope with the new illumination. An artificial gravity seemed to be coming back on. A moment later he was back on the floor, right side up, and sitting next to the command chair.

There were moans and coughs from all around, but they had air again, though it was weak like the new gravity. And as he looked around he saw that the bridge complement was back to normal.

Almost to normal. There was one exception.

A new man.

No, not a man ... an alien. Manlike, but still alien. Kirk stared at him in disbelief, and the wonder stemmed not from its alienness, but its familiarity.

Was it possible that this was all illusion? That before dying a man underwent a period of mirage-ridden temporary insanity?

The creature standing before him was half-goat, half-man. No bigger than Kirk or Spock. he was complete down to goat's horns, cloven hooves, and short, flicking tail—the compendium of all the old terran myths. Wide-shouldered and smoothly muscular, he wore a short beard and nothing else, save the thick fleece that covered him from waist to toe.

177

In human terms the goat-man appeared to be about fifty years old. That probably meant nothing, of course. But exactly how far off in his age-estimate Kirk actually was, he would not have believed.

The apparition was surveying them all with a mild, slightly bemused grin. All his movements hinted at constant delight and endless energy. And there was a strange, dancing glint in his eyes.

"Ah, humans!" came an earthquake voice that thundered around the bridge. "Lovely, primitive humans. Can't you do anything right?"

Kirk was aware the goat-man was looking down at him. He started to try and stand, but the effort was too much in the still tenuous atmosphere. "Please . . ." The deck felt like a coffin-bottom. "We need better air than this, and normal gravity . . ." His plea trailed off in a racking cough.

"Of course, of course. I was so pleased to see you—thoughtless of me. A moment."

He raised both hands over his head and brought them together with a deafening slap. Lightning flashed between his palms and formed a crackling, floating ball in the air nearby, pulsing with internal energies.

Stroking his beard with one hand, the goat-man studied the ball-lightning as it formed a complex diagram of pure energy. Then he nodded approvingly. Jabbing a finger into its center, he stirred the energy like paste. At the same time, the thundering voice sounded a single word.

"RADAMANTHUS!"

The energy diagram shattered, the flaring shards swirling around the tip of his moving finger. They collapsed to a pinpoint and vanished. A rising hum was interspersed with a series of loud clicks—something Kirk had heard few times before. Dead bridge relays snapping over as they were reactivated! The lights suddenly returned to normal, as did the gravity. And there was a sweetness in the air Kirk never thought to smell again.

Spock looked over to the library station. Computer lights once again flashed in ready patterns, indicating operational status. Arex stared in wonder at the navigation console. The instrumentation was registering again ... though as yet their readings were still incomprehensible. No doubt they meant *something*, but Arex had no reference tables for this ... place.

Even the viewscreen shone with its accustomed brilliance, once more displaying a panorama of the red-and-white world suspended below them.

Spock climbed to his feet. He took a deep, experimental breath, showing every sign of expecting his body to fly apart with the force of the inhalation.

When nothing so cataclysmic happened, he tried another, and another, then nodded in satisfaction. He was operational again, too.

Kirk also smiled in relief when, on climbing to his feet, he also found he was in good repair. Nothing seemed to be broken. And how marvelous it was just to be able to breathe. He walked to the command chair, resumed his seat.

McCoy, however, chose to remain seated on the deck. He was not going anywhere for several minutes.

Evidently quite pleased with himself, the goat-man remained standing in the middle of this renewed activity. Smiling, he began to walk around the bridge, staring curiously at this or that instrument, occasionally nodding sagely to himself or letting out a chuckle of amusement.

Eventually he stopped and turned to look back at Kirk, hands on hips.

"Everything is working again, my friends?"

"It is," admitted a confused Spock, after a rapid check of his readouts, "but it should not be. It cannot be. It is not ... logical."

Olympian laughter rolled and boomed around the

bridge as the goat-man threw back his head and roared.

"You are amused?" Spock inquired politely.

"Logical!" The goat-man grinned at him. "To whose logic do you refer, my elfin friend?"

"Look around you, Spock," advised McCoy, still sitting on the deck and enjoying life again. "Everything is working, including you and me." He made pacifying gestures with his hands at the first officer. "Let's not try to argue this gentleman out of his miracles, hmmm? It may be illogical for us to be alive now, but I'm willing to concede the situation."

"Be happy, Mr. Spock," the goat-man suggested. He ignored the first officer's continued bewilderment and spread his arms in a gesture of warm welcome. He was embracing all of them—spiritually, at least.

And he seemed at least as pleased by their good health and presence as they were by his.

"Welcome, welcome. I knew eventually humans would come searching for me—you always do. We meet again. A toast!" He reached into nearby air, and a huge tankard suddenly appeared in his hand.

Smaller versions popped into being in the hands of everyone else. The goat-man gestured to them all with his, proceeded to drain it with undisguised gusto.

Sulu took a hesitant sip from his own. His eyes lit up. He commenced to drink deeply from it. His example was quickly imitated by his shipmates.

The now-empty tankard vanishing conveniently from his hand, the goat-man moved over and helped McCoy gently to his feet. McCoy had an opportunity to study the alien at close range. By the time he stood upright again, he was satisfied that their visitor wore no clever costume. He was real, from the tip of his horns to the cleft in his hooves.

Those hooves clacked sharply on the deck as the goat-man stepped back. Now he put an arm around Spock, brought him over to McCoy and embraced both of them like long-lost brothers.

"I don't want to be impolite," Kirk began, "especially after what you've done for us ... but who are you?"

"Who am I? Oh, you want a name! Call me Baal." He paused thoughtfully. "Or Lucien. Yes, Lucien. But above all, call me friend." One finger fluttered skyward as he declaimed, "Never could I abandon those who have come so far to frolic with me ... for such purpose you must have been sent."

He surveyed the bridge again, speaking before Kirk could tell him that their motive for being here was somewhat different and not exactly voluntary.

"But not here, no, no. This is not a proper place. Let us leave this vessel and repair to where more daring delights lie." His hands moved over his head, a complicated swirling movement that left behind a trial of fading amber light, like moving lights in a time-lapse picture.

There was an explosion of dull red light, and then the swirling trails had vanished.

So had Kirk, Spock, Dr. McCoy—and the creature that called itself Lucien.

Sulu stared at the blank places on the bridge. He walked to the spot where the ship's doctor had stood seconds before, moved his hands through the air over the place like a blind man searching for unknown things.

Uhura watched him, her face showing fear and bewilderment, while Arex sat motionless by the operative but still useless navigation console.

In a sense, they were still drifting in darkness ...

Only a last word or two lingered in Sulu's mind, the last thing the goat-man had said before disappearing. Or were they words—or only meaningless nonsense syllables of an alien argot which his brain automatically arranged into human-sounding groups?

"Megas-tu ..." the goat-man had said.

Kirk felt himself floating, floating. A globe turned slowly, patiently beneath him, came nearer. He saw that its red-and-white candy stripes were vast cloud formations. They were in constant motion crashing and rolling against one another, sometimes blending into various shades of pink, sometimes forming sharp lines between. Red battled white here as the sea battled the land on more familiar worlds.

They drifted further, closer—for he could see other shapes floating with him—and suddenly were within the banded atmosphere. The crimson and cream bands kept their color as he descended, and for the first time he saw what caused the redness. Miles-high storms of brilliant red dust and sand colored the clouds.

Then the surface became visible, an unstable, swirling chaos of constantly changing shape and form. Only occasional isolated hints of something solid beneath him indicated that this planet possessed a real surface. Even so, he felt there was nothing to prevent them from drifting right through that flowing "ground" until they came out the other side of the world.

As soon as he thought he had finally fixed a stable point on the surface, it would break apart and dissolve into nothingness, or explode in a pinwheel of color.

Nothing was finite here; nothing was constant; nothing was real. Even the air had color, the wind producing harsh cries and strange slithering sounds as of creatures and cloth brushing against one another.

The soul-filled breeze blew red-and-white particles into miniature dust-storms that twisted and writhed into insane alien shapes.

In the midst of this anarchy, four people appeared.

Kirk was one of them, Spock and McCoy two others, Lucien the fourth. The three officers immediately covered their eyes. Until they had actually touched down the three officers had seemed to be at once a part of and apart from the elements. Now the wind had a chillness to it, and the flying sand abraded unprotected flesh.

They shielded their faces as best they could and tried to see around them. There was no discernable horizon. Lucien stood nearby, impassive, waiting, watching.

"Spock, Bones—you all right?" Kirk managed to shout. The sound of his own voice in this place was reassuring.

"Nothing more serious than a faceful of sand, Jim," McCoy responded. "But I wish I had a medical tricorder, just to check in case we—" He broke off. Kirk turned, saw through separated fingers that the doctor was staring at him. That wasn't surprising; he found himself staring in fascination back at McCoy.

"Jim, look at yourself!"

Kirk felt no change—and yet there was something. He looked at himself, as instructed, and saw fingers parting from hands, hands from wrists, wrists from arms, and arms from shoulders. All of his limbs were drifting away from the central torso, drifting away and changing shape. He saw his trunk splitting up into neat, irregular blobs, still fully clothed. There was no pain, merely the quiet astonishing sight of bits of himself coming apart, like a jigsaw puzzle in water.

The same thing was happening to Spock and McCoy. Their bodies were coming apart in toy-like bits and pieces, floating away from one another, sections of loose Spock mixing with fragments of McCoy.

Little bits of the *Enterprise*'s first officer tumbled lazily past Kirk. The painless amputations were changing themselves, now stretching out like rubber, now growing thick and fat, as they wobbled along.

Spock stared in fascination as his left arm elongated and turned into a flowing rivulet of colored sand.

"Lucien, do something!" Kirk yelled.

"But why, Captain?" The goat-man shook his head pityingly, suddenly remembering. "Oh, very well. I'd forgotten how much bodily integrity means to you poor humans." Kirk noticed that the goat-man had also come apart, though it didn't appear to bother him.

A swirling cloud of dust formed one of Lucien's hands, fully equipped with a proper complement of fingers. It moved, and something like a neon pentagram appeared in the air, floating, glowing radiantly. There was a flash of brilliant crimson again—Lucien seemed fond of red, or perhaps that was simply the common color of manipulated energy here—from each point of the five-cornered shape. It was repeated once, twice, and twice again.

Five drifting globes of flame touched the free particles, squeezing them together, reshaping and rejoining the mixed forms and making them whole again.

Kirk saw his arms, legs, lower torso reform, move, and join together again neatly and painlessly. Abruptly, the drifting flame winked out. The pentagram itself followed shortly, vanishing into the all-consuming wind.

Kirk reached down and cautiously felt himself. He pulled experimentally at his right wrist with his left—not altogether sure how he would react if the hand came off. Around him, the rest of the impossible world still remained shapeless, all rolling mists and roarings and whines arising out of nothingness.

Lucien sighed. Probably in deference to his guests, he had reformed his own corpus. "This isn't easy, you know, holding us all together like this. It's not even natural."

"If you know as much about us as you claim to," said a much relieved McCoy, "you'll know that being in one piece is very natural where we come from."

"Really, Doctor?" Spock commented. "Personally, I find all this quite absorbing."

"Yes, but that's probably because you're not natural to begin with, Spock."

Suddenly, a pair of long green tentacles, like the arms of an octopus, appeared out of the coiling mists and brushed against the face of a startled Kirk. Instinctively, he jerked away, and they vanished.

"Look, Lucien," he began, as much to take his mind off the disturbing apparition as to obtain information, "or whatever you want to call yourself—I want to know why you brought us here." Even as he said the words he was fully aware that if the goat-man chose to ignore the question they could do nothing to compel him to answer.

It made no difference whether he was inclined to or not. Before their savior/captor could reply, a tremendous roaring sprang up like the wildest of hurricanes. A frenzied wind whipped up around them. It lifted Kirk and dashed him to the ground, which conveniently became soft sand beneath him just in time to cushion the impact.

Lucien frowned and made another of his cryptic gestures. Red and rose energy flashed from his fingertips. The hurricane wind died as abruptly as it had arisen. Lucien finished his complicated hand-weaving in the air.

Even as they watched, the landscape shimmered, altered, and began to take on form and substance. Then they were standing on a grassy knoll, complete with weeds, trees, and a running stream. The knoll was cloaked in heather and milkweed. Kirk became aware of a new figure standing next to him. He looked down.

A small goat-boy stared back at him. A dancing miniature whirlwind spun in his open palm—the hurricane which had just thrown Kirk so callously around. The toy tornado slowed, slowed, and became a child's top. It stopped and fell over in the boy's hand.

Lucien bestowed a mildly disapproving smile on the youngster. "Kids will play." The boy grinned back, clutched tightly at his top, and hurried off to the top of the knoll.

Kirk picked himself up off the grass, pulling up a small tuft of it as he rose, and examined the newly materialized growth. It looked and smelled like good old earth-type field clover. But he wouldn't have batted an eye if it had suddenly turned into a twelve-legged Denebian spider.

Lucien was still busy. He dropped his hands to his sides and brought them up slowly, trembling, toward the sky. The forest rose close around them in rhythm with his rising hands, everything from bushes and seedlings to mature trees.

There was a gap in the woods, and Lucien gestured toward it, pointing to a vast structure that one moment was kilometers away, the next, close enough to reach out and touch.

"Is this better, my friends? You must remember it has been a long, long time since I've associated with anything human. I hope memory serves well enough. I have tried to translate my world into symbols your minds can comprehend. I could have altered your minds to perceive mine, instead, but I seem to recall that you frown on such things."

No one claimed otherwise.

By then they were all gazing toward the gap in the trees, toward the now-near, now-distant city.

It was a fairyland of crystal and ceramic mosaic, of glass and free-sculpted metals—a fairyland into which the forest, by all laws of perspective, should have extended, yet did not.

On open streets, men and women and children walked through neatly paved ways, each person differently dressed, all elaborately caped and gowned.

"Welcome, my friends, to Megas-tu," Lucien declaimed happily. "Welcome to you, and you, and you." He said it proudly, like an old man showing off his favorite grandson.

Kirk turned from the incredible metropolis back to the goat-man. "And what is Megas-tu? I would have said a world, but I've seen too much in the past few hours, or weeks, or whatever the time-referent is here, to accept anything merely on what I see."

"It is merely that, Captain James Kirk. A world. A world that operates on rules different from those of your universe." He snapped the fingers of one hand, and they found themselves seated on the grass in front of a flowing brook.

Brocaded cloths were spread all around. Quantities of sweet-smelling food and drink showed from under the lids of bulging wicker baskets. It was all very beautiful and nice and horrifying.

Lucien noticed the ambivalent expressions of his guests, looked thoughtful. "Let me see ... it takes a moment for me to remember some of your terms, you know. What is the word?" He paused a moment, then brightened.

"Ah yes, magic. Our universe operates according to the precepts of what you superstitiously call magic. Our laws are not unrealistic—merely different." He plucked an apple from empty air, took a bite out of it, and caught another. He tossed it to McCoy.

The doctor caught it automatically. "I know this is just a figment of my imagination, but—" He took a sample nibble, smiled in approval.

"It is, as you see, quite real, Dr. McCoy," Lucien continued. "Everything here is real, if you only try to see. For example . . ." He seemed to search the deserted knoll for a moment, then gestured.

An intricately decorated tent decorated with cabalistic symbols appeared on the grass a short distance away. An attractive girl, as delicate as Chinese porcelain, moved to enter the tent. She paused at the entrance, which was opened by an old, wrinkled woman.

They were still too far away for the watchers from the *Enterprise* to overhear their conversation, but some kind of business transaction seemed to be taking place. After a few minutes of this, the old woman nodded and disappeared inside. She came out shortly thereafter holding a small stoppered bottle.

Lucien spoke while the two women—if such they really were—resumed their conversation. "Beautiful, isn't she? But all our women are as young and appealing as they want to be. When anyone can be as lovely as her aesthetics demand, character soon takes over from vanity. Hence the potion-seller prefers a more traditional configuration. It makes for better business.

"To insure the man of her dreams, the young one seeks a slight edge."

"Not a love potion?" said the skeptical Kirk. "There's nothing magical about that. It's just a question of chemistry."

Lucien gave him an odd look. "You must have made some progress in certain areas since I last visited your people, Captain." He gestured, and the tent scene vanished.

Another exchange was taking place off to their right, now, on what should have been the empty top of the knoll. Two human shapes were conversing there. One was a tall, thin gentleman clad in flowing robes and a conical hat inscribed with mystic devices. He stood stroking his long white beard, deep in discussion with a manlike creature that sported a pair of wings and a traditionally gargoylish face.

After some minutes of this, the tall man in the robes turned and gestured with his hands. There was a by-now familiar crackling in the air, and sparks of loose energy grew from nothingness. They lengthened, joined together, forming beams and walls and ceilings.

The clashing colors coalesced into four solid uprights. Gesturing and prancing all the while, the oldster danced around them, solidifying the small building. It rose lithe, delicate, with high ornamental spires and turrets and smooth polished domes.

Eventually the robed dancer came to a halt. Hands on hips, he studied the finished project, then nodded in satisfaction at his completed handiwork. A last gesture, and a sign appeared over the entrance to the compact castle, the inscription in an unknown calligraphy.

"Do you need a home?" asked Lucien. "A stable, a town? Stop in and visit your friendly sorcerer-contractor. Let him do the hard work."

"Sorcerer," Spock muttered. "Of course. Federation scientists were more correct than they suspected. In order to function, any supranormal spatial phenomenon must extend through known space and time to another dimensional plane.

"The interaction of interdimensional forces supplies the energy to produce new galactic matter. It explains not only our expanding universe, but also why the physical laws here differ so completely from our own."

"I'm not sure I follow all that, Spock, but are you saying you believe in magic?"

Spock looked back at him unwaveringly. "I believe in what is logical and what follows from observable facts, Doctor. The basic laws here appear to be what we sometimes call 'magic.' The *Enterprise* does not operate according to these principles, therefore it ceased to function. And so, almost, did we."

"So you used magic," guessed Kirk, turning to face Lucien, "to get our ship working again."

"It was the natural thing to do, Captain. You could have done it yourself, with a little instruction. But then, few of you humans ever bothered to become proficient at magic." He frowned slightly. "Those among you who did were not looked upon with favor. Some of you even managed to reach all the way through to Megas-tu through small interdimensional vortices."

"All the way from Earth to here?" exclaimed a cynical McCoy. "Impossible."

"Distances in our universe do not operate according to your laws, either, Doctor," Lucien told him. "By our methods of reckoning, certain parts of Earth are right next door."

"Lucien," interrupted Kirk, suddenly serious, "you persist in calling us friends, implying that you know us. Even more, that we should know you. But how?"

"Ah, Captain, Captain!" The goat-man leaned back on the grass and rested his head in his hands, staring at the blue sky. "To feign such ignorance with *me*. Still, it *was* always one of my problems." He stopped, and Kirk got the impression he had somehow hurt the goat-man's feelings.

Lucien crawled forward then and swept his hand through the clear surface of the brook. His fingers broke the water once and withdrew.

"Listen, look, I'll try to explain further."

The ripples stilled. Colors began to appear, staining the clearness. Shapes started to form, and soon it was like looking into a viewscreen. Gone completely was the sandy bottom of the stream. In its place they saw a broad panorama of men and women—Megans—exotic and familiar, chiseled handsome and intentionally plain, all sitting lost in contemplation amid the howling chaos that was the real surface of Megas-tu.

"This may seem to you humans to be a world of insanity and instability," declared Lucien. "But it has the quality of change we all demand. My people are calm and contented, each one existing in the world of his or her imagination."

The image in the screen blurred, changed, and Kirk and his companions had again a view of the Megan universe as they first encountered it, a riot of blending colors and splinters of stellar shape.

"There are no rivals in our little universe at all, Captain Kirk. No other life-forms save ourselves." The picture jumped again, and they were back on Megas-tu. As they watched, the people in the stream-picture stood together, and some of them began to rise upward, free of the planet.

"Millennia ago," Lucien continued, "in our search for companionship, we Megans passed through the various gates between dimensions, including the great vortex you entered by.

"Eventually, on one such expedition, we discovered," and the scene shifted again as if anticipating his words, "your world—Earth." They now saw a view of the blue-white globe of Terra, seen from space. Kirk felt an unexpected quickening. He had been away from home for too long.

"Wherever we went we became friends and advisors to mankind. To help your ancestors out of their misery and ignorance we drew as best we could on the power left behind in our own universe, bringing it in through tiny gates." Hands stirred the water again, and ripples blotted out the blue-white ball.

When the stream had stilled once more, Kirk saw only the sandy bottom and a couple of dreamlike shadows cast by small fish.

Lucien sat back and shook the droplets from his hand. "Eventually we were forced to leave," he concluded. "It was a group decision. For myself, I wanted to stay. Ah, how I fought, how I argued! You see, I was the generalist, the apologist among specialists."

"The troublemaker, the others said. But I'd grown to love Earth and its unpredictable, funny people." He saw visions of the past. "Those were the days ... you crazy, irrational humans." He looked over at them.

"But now you have come back to me. It is so good to see you again." He leaped to his feet, a gesture of pure joy, and sprang into a hectic, prancing dance, to the accompaniment of a cheerful piping that seemed to come from all around them.

The music was infectious, and Kirk found himself smiling as he spoke. "If you Megans enjoyed Earth so much, why did you leave it? I don't understand ..."

"Captain, good Captain, always so curious, always there must be a reason," the dancing Lucien laughed. "Another reason why I liked you humans so much.

The vortex knows you have many special qualities—
and special faults."

He took a giant leap and whirled in the air, performing an outrageous multiple pirouette that carried him
to the tops of the highest trees . . . where he froze motionless. There was a new note in his voice when he
spoke, a hint of concern, of worry, that was alien to the
Lucien they had started to know.

"No." The piping melody faded into silence, and he
was down at their side again in a second. His boyish
pleasure had turned desperately serious.

"You must go."

"What is it?" asked a nervous McCoy. "What's
wrong?"

"I cannot tell you just now. But you must return to
your vessel immediately. And quiet, be quiet about it.
You must not give your presence away."

Kirk tried for elaboration, but Lucien was already
gesturing again. A rainbow haze blurred Kirk's vision,
and he felt himself rising, rising and dissolving . . .

Scott, Sulu and Uhura were clustered anxiously on
the bridge, all crowded around the main navigation console where Arex was struggling to make some sense out
of the computer readouts. Their study was shattered by
a sudden crackling behind them, and they turned
quickly.

Pulsing with vast power held carefully in check, a
red-and-white cloud appeared in the center of the
bridge. It broke into three smaller clouds, which gradually contracted into the shapes of Kirk, McCoy, and
Spock.

Everyone on the bridge rushed forward to the returned officers, all trying to speak at once.

"Captain Kirk . . . what happened? . . . where were
you all? . . . given you up, Mr. Spock . . ."

"One at a time, one at a time," Kirk admonished

them, making calming motions. "We're ... we're all right." He took a deep breath, looked around him.

They were back on the *Enterprise*, and it had never looked quite so good. After the mad maelstrom below, the clean lines of the bridge were reassuring—even if they held their shape only through Lucien's will. And it was good to be back among *real* people again. Though the look in Uhura's eyes ...

"Status report, first."

"Everythin's okay, it seems, Captain. All systems except the warp-engines are workin' perfectly, and I can have them operatin' in two or three hours. But you ..."

"The only thing that's wrong with me, Mr. Scott, is that I'm still badly confused by a number of things."

"You've got plenty of company, Jim," McCoy noted. "What did Lucien mean, we're not to 'give ourselves away'? Give ourselves away to whom? Couldn't anyone else on Megas-tu detect us up here? I would think we kind of stand out."

"They'd need mighty powerful scanners to find us now," said Scott, who was ignorant of the realities of Megas. "See that?" He indicated the main viewscreen.

A thick layer of dense, particle-laden material now lay like luminescent gray smoke between the *Enterprise* and the surface, blotting out the red-and-white clouds below them.

"It's somethin' like a big dust cloud, Captain," said Scott, "and yet it's different. Been between us and the surface ever since you disappeared. Communicator and scanner beams wouldn't penetrate ... we tried." Kirk swiveled to face the library station.

"If it was Lucien who put it there, Captain," Spock mused, "the question then becomes ... why is he hiding us? What danger are we in from something on his world?" Kirk nodded, turned back to his chief engineer.

"Weapon's status, Mr. Scott? It seems we may have to be ready to defend ourselves."

"Then it'll have to be with fast talk, Captain. Our phaser banks and defensive screens require at least a partial powering-up of the warp-drive engines. Give me a few hours and I might be able to say different."

"Do the best you can, Scotty." Kirk's voice dropped to a murmur. "We can't defend ourselves and we can't run away. And we don't even know what it is we might have to fight. So," and he clapped both hands firmly to the arms of the command chair, "we wait."

"And do what?" wondered McCoy aloud. "Lucien may not show up again for three hundred years, our time. By then, I might be an old man."

"I have an interesting idea," proposed a calm voice. They all turned their attention to Spock. "Captain, I think it would be best to first try this in private. If you will accompany me to my quarters? And Dr. McCoy as well?"

"What have you got in mind, Spock?"

"Something in the nature of an experiment, Captain. It may prove quite interesting. And if we are fortunate, practical as well."

The door slid quietly aside as the three officers entered Spock's spacious room. Kirk and McCoy watched as Spock moved to his desk and fished out a thick, white marking stylus. He waved them to one side.

"A little room, please, gentlemen." They stepped back and stood against the far wall.

While they watched with growing curiosity, Spock proceeded to sketch a rough pentagram on the smooth floor, erasing one arm and redrawing it when it seemed too much longer than the others. Kirk and McCoy recognized the pentagram shape, something that made no sense in connection with Spock. The latter clarified his actions as soon as the diagram was finished.

"Not being a logical corollary of physics, magic was never subjected to quite the serious study on Vulcan as it received on Earth. No doubt the actions of visiting Megans lent it somewhat more credibility on your world. Some of your more credulous philosophers—or more perceptive—went as far as to attempt to codify the most formal principles of the so-called 'dark arts.' In the course of my readings on Earth I had occasion to encounter much information of this sort." He got to his feet, gazed thoughtfully down at the pentagram.

"I believe this is one of the most important and basic mystical symbols described by the terran 'magicians.' I observed Lucien utilizing the same device earlier." Kirk began to see where Spock was heading.

"Lucien did say something to the effect that we could master the same techniques," Kirk pondered. "Spock, you're saying that as long as we're in this universe, we can 'work' magic, too?"

"One must always be prepared to employ the resources at hand, Captain." He hesitated. "Although I must confess it requires considerable effort for me to readjust my thinking along such lines." He walked into the center of the pentagram.

"Watch there, now." He pointed toward his desk. An elaborate three-dimensional maze laden with double-toned crystal pieces sat on one end.

"I will attempt to move one of the Vulcan chess pieces using only magic—magic in our universe, but what should merely be the proper utilization of a local scientific principle."

"But how can you, Spock?" McCoy objected. "I mean, you don't know the words, or the proper gestures, or—"

"It should be the mental state that counts, Doctor. And I have the terran magical principles to use for a base." He gestured for quiet, assumed a stance of deep concentration.

Stretching out his arms toward the table, he began to speak. "May the energy of this universe be the power in me." Kirk and McCoy stared expectantly, hopefully, at the chess set. There was no hint of movement.

"Forget it, Spock," advised McCoy after several

minutes of intense concentration on the first officer's part had proven ineffectual. "It won't work."

Spock lowered his arms slightly and opened his eyes. "It *has* to work, Doctor. It is logical it should work—here." He closed his eyes halfway and tried again.

"I draw on your energy . . . I know I can. I *believe* I can. For every action, yea, let there be an equal and opposite reaction."

There was a sudden crackling in the air. McCoy jumped halfway out of his regulation boots. Yellow and black fire flashed around Spock's body. A thin sliver of energy leaped from one of his hands to the table.

It touched a Vulcan rook, enveloped it in yellow flame, and moved it three spaces forward. Kirk smiled.

"Well now. Let me try that, Spock." Spock obligingly stepped out of the pentagram and let Kirk take his place.

He raised his arms hesitantly toward the table, looked over at his first officer for reassurance. "This feels ridiculous, Mr. Spock."

"The important thing is to relax and concentrate, Captain. I think the physical gesture is purely supplementary . . . a psychological crutch. Merely a way of helping the mind focus thought. Like talking out loud."

"Now really, Jim," began McCoy. "You can't expect to fully duplicate . . ."

McCoy was cut off by the rumble of a small thunderclap echoing through the room. But the doctor was right. Kirk could not duplicate Spock's results . . . exactly.

The colors that flashed around him were not yellow and black, but blue and green, sea-color fire. One fringe of it nudged a bishop two spaces, then lifted and dropped it down a level.

"Good move, Captain," commented Spock idly. Kirk dropped his arms and stared at the chessboard, still not quite able to believe he had done it.

Sudden enthusiasm replaced McCoy's skepticism. "Wait a minute now—it's my turn."

"Only two at a time can play the game, Doctor. I believe we can find other, more interesting uses, for this extraordinary ability. With a little practice, it should be possible to control the local energy flow without the use of clumsy inscribed symbols such as this pentagram."

The demonstration that Kirk, Spock, and McCoy gave on the bridge caused the expected sensation, but the surprise and shock soon gave way to delight as Sulu, Uhura, and the others discovered they too could manipulate the Megan magic.

Not having a chess set handy, they followed Spock's suggestion and practiced with the bridge instrumentation. Kirk discovered that he was able to activate or deactivate the main viewscreen with a simple gesture. But he could not work the magnification controls. Apparently the more delicate the instrument, the finer one's grasp of the energies involved had to be.

"Hey, where's Scotty?" asked McCoy suddenly, looking around the bridge.

"I think he headed up to the recreation room on B-deck," Sulu replied absently. He was making elaborate twisting movements, but so far had achieved nothing more than a floating cloud of writhing energy a meter in front of his hands.

"Now what do you think he'd want in there, do you suppose?" wondered Kirk.

Scott surveyed the recreation room to make certain it was empty. Then he moved to the unit games dispenser and requested a normal tennis ball. But he didn't go through the door leading to the indoor court.

Instead, he made a number of swinging, swerving gestures with both hands. Energy appeared out of air and formed a glowing nimbus around the ball. It was abruptly sucked up by the spheroid, acting as a vacuum. The ball quivered as Scott concentrated on it, then dropped to the floor, bounced once and ricocheted off the far wall.

Beautifully executed—except Scott had overlooked one small factor. The ball was moving at about a hundred kilometers an hour, and showed no sign of slowing down.

It struck the roof and rocketed toward Scott. Showing some impressive speed of his own, the chief engineer dove under a nearby game table. The ball contacted the floor near his left foot, shot across the room, hit the far wall, bounced back up to the ceiling, the floor again, across the rooom—and it appeared to be picking *up* speed.

Seconds later it whizzed past his head, and Scott hurriedly covered his face with his hands. Crouched in that awkward position he wiggled his fingers desperately. It had not the slightest effect on the ball, which continued to whizz around the room like a runaway warp-engine. It was now moving so fast Scott could see it only as a weak blur.

Scottish magic can be very strong.

Back up on the bridge, Sulu had assumed a look of grim determination. He made a last, twisting thrust at the drifting ball of energy he had conjured up. Abruptly it darkened, coalesced, and formed into the most beautiful girl in this or any other universe.

He had been expecting it all along—the helmsman was a positive thinker. He moved forward, arms extended to embrace her . . . but when his lips touched, the image dissolved.

"I've heard of devastating kissers," said the watching McCoy, "but don't you think that's overdoing it a little, Sulu?"

"Very funny, Doctor," Sulu moved his hands again, slowly constructing another human shape out of colored fire.

The officers of the *Enterprise* continued to practice their new-found talents. Eventually Kirk found that he could make the viewscreen do just about anything it could do in normal space-time, only here he did not have to touch a single control.

On B-deck, the whining ball finally came to a sudden halt. Scott looked out warily from under the table. First the covering and finally the interior material had disintegrated—shredded by sheer speed. But not before the ball had managed to put some respectable dents in the metal walls.

Eyeing the now defunct remnants of the ball with respect, he moved back to the games producer ... and ordered a set of checkers. This time he would practice with something a little less lethal.

Sulu was sweating with effort and had managed to generate another girl. He leaned toward her again. This time his curious audience included several other members of the bridge complement, who had left off their own practicing to watch him.

"Good luck," Uhura volunteered.

Sulu kissed the apparition ... and the girl's arms went around him as she kissed back. His eyes bugged in surprise. That he hadn't expected. But he recovered quickly, returned the kiss with fervor—too much fervor. The energy-waif burst into little match-flares and was gone.

Sulu was prepared to try yet a third time, but a red-and-white cloud suddenly filled the center of the bridge. It faded, and once more Lucien stood among them. But this time he was not grinning or dancing. In fact, he looked agitated and upset.

"What are you doing?" He gazed around in anxious confusion. Kirk looked back at him.

"Learning to protect ourselves, Lucien."

"Protect yourselves? Is that all human beings ever think about—fighting? I'll take care of you. That's what friends are for." He started pacing back and forth.

"I don't know ... I just don't know. All this mental

energy you've been using. Your peculiar patterns . . . it can be traced, you know. You might be found."

A voice thunderous enough to dwarf Lucien's suddenly filled the bridge, accompanied by the whistling, howling, spine-twisting moans of the real, uncontrolled Megas-tu.

"HAVE BEEN FOUND!" it rumbled.

Lucien halted in mid-step. Kirk was startled to see something very like fear appear in the face of the up to now omnipotent goat-man. For the first time it occurred to Kirk that Lucien might not have exceptional powers among his own kind.

He didn't care to think what sort of being might.

But it seemed they were about to find out.

A new cloud of colors began to form on the bridge. There was more of the fiery black this time—yellow, white, electric blues and orange, swirling and reforming and curling; all the slithery nightmare shapes of the world below seemed present in that cloud.

A scare-thing, all crooked teeth and bulging eyes, grew out of the floor in front of Lucien. It blended back into the cloud as Uhura screamed.

"SO THE PEOPLE OF EARTH WOULD SPREAD THEIR EVILS EVEN UNTO OUR HOME? WE ARE READY THIS TIME FOR HUMAN PERFIDY. THIS TIME IT IS THE HUMANS WHO SHALL SUFFER . . . FOR HERE OUR POWER IS ABSOLUTE."

"THE HUMANS . . . AND YOU, LUCIEN," and the voice mocked the goat-man, "SHALL BE THE ONES TO PAY." It rose to a bansheelike wail on the last syllable, and stopped.

There was a powerful wrench, a jerk, and everyone had to grab quickly at something fixed to keep from being thrown to the deck. Kirk's gaze went immediately to the viewscreen.

The glowing gray cloud that had blocked them off from the planet had vanished. The *Enterprise* was dropping like a rock toward the angry surface below. It seemed certain they were going to smash to splinters on the packed sands, but the starship suddenly slowed, touched the ground awkwardly. A howling storm of rainbow-colored rain began to pour into the ship.

It was followed by fiery hailstones that rained down upon them as though the hull didn't exist. Everyone was knocked to the floor, including Lucien.

"Keep calm!" Kirk yelled dazedly, above the rattle of strangely soft hailstones.

An ominous rumbling sounded, and the *Enterprise* started to shake . . . slowly at first, then rapidly, until Kirk felt like an ingredient in a cake mix.

A shattering crack sounded, and the *Enterprise* split neatly down the middle, like a grape. Then the two halves of the starship started to change shape, to break up as Kirk, Spock, and McCoy had broken up at their first touch-down on Megas-tu. Smaller and smaller pieces detached and broke away, floating off into the screaming winds.

But this time the reforming was different. The floating bits of *Enterprise* regrouped to form, not the starship, but buildings—buildings lining a street that looked much like an old terran village. Very old.

"Seventeenth century," mumbled Kirk as he rematerialized. He felt himself caught in an awkward bent-over position, his hands fixed up by his ears. He was fixed, he saw, in an ancient wooden device. Looking to his left, right, and across the street, he saw the entire crew of the *Enterprise*, set into similar stocks.

Row on row of the T-post structures faded into distant haze. Scott was trapped close by, as were Spock, McCoy, and Lucien. Kirk seemed to be at one end of the long line of imprisoned crew.

He turned his head to the right. There was a crudely engraved sign set in the ground beside a gnarled old oak.

SALEM, MASS., the sign said. It keyed no response in Kirk.

The world shimmered and dissolved again. Once more Kirk felt himself pulled lazily apart, reformed. Town and crew vanished. Dust walls formed around him, mortared with flickering bursts of energy.

Higher and higher the walls rose, solidifying into a huge, aged meeting hall, obviously terran in origin. But the scale was wrong. The room was big . . . much too big.

He was still bound in the wooden stocks, but a bench had been produced to sit on. He looked around once more and found Spock staring back at him.

"I know, Mr. Spock. Sixteenth-or-seventeenth-century terran architecture, I'd guess—with the size all out of proportion."

Spock tried to turn his head toward the Captain. "I saw the sign, also. If I recall your history correctly, Salem was a small town on the east coast of the North American continent. As for the date, I should guess approximately 1691."

" 'Approximately'?" echoed Kirk. "Why 1691?"

The first officer didn't reply. Instead, he concentrated on the seemingly endless tiers of seats facing them, seats that extended back and up to absurd distances. Perspective as well as proportion seemed distorted here.

The seats were beginning to fill with men and women, all clad in costumes of the same period as the hall.

Since everyone in the stocks was a member of the ship's crew, excepting Lucien, both Kirk and Spock concluded quickly that those filling the endless balcony were the Megans themselves. The reason for taking on human shape seemed obvious. The reason for the particular period costumes did not.

There were hundreds, then thousands of them, and still they poured in, becoming tiny with increasing distance. Even so, Kirk found he could distinguish those in the furthest rows with perfect clarity. It made no sense—but he was beginning to accept such things as normal for Megas-tu.

The arrivals were talking solemnly among themselves. But when the last, uppermost seat had been filled, the buzz of low conversation died as if on signal.

A pause, and then a brilliant flare of light in the center of the room, before the first stocks. A last Megan appeared there, in human form. A tall, glowering man, wearing a wide-brimmed black hat.

The man surveyed the crew of the *Enterprise*, pinioned tightly in their wooden restraints, then turned to the watching Megans. His voice was deep, powerful . . . and familiar.

It was the voice that had erupted on the bridge only moments . . . days, years . . . before.

"WE ARE GATHERED HERE TODAY, GOOD CITIZENS, TO SEE JUSTICE DONE. YOU MUST BE THE JUDGES. THESE . . ." and he indicated those in the stocks, "ARE THE DE-FENDANTS.

"AS REPRESENTATIVES OF THE VILEST SPECIES IN THE UNIVERSE . . . TRECHEROUS HUMANITY . . . THEY ARE TO BE JUDGED." He moved forward and stopped to stare grimly down at Lucien. ". . . AND THOSE WHO WOULD AID THEM." He turned away.

"AS SPECIALIST IN THE ETHICS OF MAGIC, I HAVE BEEN APPOINTED PROSECUTOR HERE." He started a complicated gesture, but Kirk, fighting with the unyielding wood, interrupted.

"If this is a trial, I think we've got the right to know what you're already so convinced we've done."

The tall prosecutor, who could have obliterated Kirk in a bust of yellow flame, nodded in agreement. He pointed toward Lucien.

"HAS THIS ONE NOT TOLD YOU HOW WE VISITED EARTH, AND WHAT WAS DONE TO US THERE?"

"Lucien said only that you came as wise men, wizards who . . ."

The Prosecutor leaned forward, shaking an angry fist.

"THEN HEAR THIS. ONCE, UPON YOUR WORLD, I WAS KNOWN AS ASMODEUS, WHO SEES ALL. GAZE UPON MY COUNTENANCE, SO THAT YOU, TOO, MAY KNOW THE TRUTH."

And the Prosecutor's face started to come apart. It expanded, flattened, became a swirling rectangular screen. A picture formed in it, the picture of the insane galaxy that roiled around Megas-tu.

Colors died to black, changed, and the view turned to one of breathtakingly normal space—space-black flecked with the brilliant points of distant stars.

Changed again, to a picture of Earth. Moved in close, closer. The Prosecutor spoke as various sequences appeared and played themselves out on the facial screen.

The first scenes depicted Megans in human guise engaged in numerous daily activities—as witches, sorcerers, and warlocks.

"WE CAME TO YOUR WORLD AS FRIENDS," the Prosecutor's voice boomed, "BUT WHEREVER WE WENT, THE STORY INVARIABLY HAD THE SAME ENDING. SOME HUMANS WOULD ATTEMPT TO USE US TO GAIN POWER, TO SERVE THEIR OWN GREED AND LUST. AND IN OUR IGNORANCE OF HUMAN WAYS, WE SOMETIMES FELL PARTY TO THESE SUBTLE INIQUITIES.

"WHEN WE DISCOVERED SUCH VENALITY AND REFUSED TO SERVE SUCH MEN, THEY TURNED THE PEOPLE AGAINST US, TAUGHT THE COMMON FOLK TO FEAR AND HATE US.

"SINCE OUR POWER IN YOUR UNIVERSE IS LIMITED, WE WERE VULNERABLE." The view changed to show Megans being driven from towns by the fearful populace, spat upon and reviled.

"THEY CALLED US DEVILS, DEMONS, CONJURERS!" the voice declaimed, rising to a shout. As it did so, the facial screen shattered into a thousand flickering particles, which faded back to nothingness.

The face of the Prosecutor reappeared.

"THOSE OF US WHO SURVIVED THESE EARLY PURGES," he continued, "DECIDED TO MAKE ONE FINAL ATTEMPT TO SECURE A HELPING COLONY ON YOUR WORLD. THEY GATHERED IN THE SMALL TOWN OF SALEM, MASSACHUSETTS.

"THERE, THOSE OF US WHO WERE LEFT DISCOVERED THAT IN TRYING TO LEARN YOUR WAYS, TO BLEND IN WITH YOU, WE HAD FORGOTTEN MUCH KNOWLEDGE. EVEN SO, WE TRIED TO HELP YOU IN THIS NEWLY SETTLED LAND, BUT . . ."

"You made mistakes," guessed Spock.

"IT IS TRUE THERE WERE OCCASIONS WHEN WE USED OUR POWERS AWKWARDLY, AND MANY OF US SUFFERED AS A RESULT OF IT. SOME OF US . . . BURNED FOR IT. BURNED! AS WITCHES."

Kirk nodded sadly. The significance of Salem had come back to him.

"WE GATHERED THE SURVIVORS OF OUR SETTLEMENT OUTSIDE THE TOWN, AND TRIED TO RECALL ENOUGH MEGAN KNOWLEDGE TO RETURN TO OUR OWN UNIVERSE, TO LEAVE YOUR HELLISH WORLD. TO RETURN TO SAFETY, COMFORT, REASON . . ."

"And loneliness," put in Lucien, "and fear, and . . ."

"SHOULD WE NOT FEAR THE EARTHLINGS?" the Prosecutor insisted. "SHOULD WE NOT FEAR THE CRUELTY OF SUCH MINDLESS PRIMITIVES? CONSIDER THE WEAPONS THEY HAVE MASTERED, AND MISUSED, SINCE WE LEFT. NEVER SINCE HAVE WE ATTEMPTED TO EXPLORE YOUR UNIVERSE," he informed them, directing his attention to Kirk and Spock.

"NEVER SINCE HAVE WE SOUGHT OUTSIDE COMPANIONSHIP, TO IMPOSE OUR HELP ON THOSE WHOSE CREEDS ARE SUPERSTITION, GREED, AND TERROR. YET, DESPITE OUR CAUTION, YOU HAVE COME HERE, TO OUR VERY HOME."

"If one Federation ship can find us, so can others," Lucien whispered to Kirk. "That is what they fear."

The Prosecutor appeared to lose some of his antagonism. In fact, his thunder now held a surprising note of sadness.

"WE DO NOT WANT TO DO THIS, CAPTAIN KIRK. WE DO NOT WANT TO HARM YOU. THE NATURE OF OUR UNIVERSE IS ONE OF CONSTANT CHANGE, EVERYTHING IS TRANSITORY. SO ARE OUR GRUDGES. WE HAVE NEVER HAD TO HURT ANYONE BEFORE.

"IF THERE WERE SOME TRUE REASON NOT TO . . ." He turned, gazed back at the uncounted thousands who filled the distorted tiers of the hall. "WHO WILL SPEAK IN DEFENSE OF MANKIND? WHO?"

A slight whisper of bodies shifting on wooden seats was the only reply.

A familiar voice on Kirk's left broke the silence. "I will, Asmodeus. I am only partly of Earth." The Prosecutor moved near, seemed to inspect Spock.

" 'TIS TRUE ENOUGH. YOU ARE DIFFERENT. IF NONE OBJECT . . ." He looked back at the crowd. Still-silence still.

"THE COURT WILL THEN HEAR A DEFENSE." A casual gesture and Spock's stocks became so much sawdust.

The first officer stumbled on cramped legs at the sudden disappearance of the bonds. Then he straightened, rubbing at ankles and wrists.

"I have had no time to prepare a formal defense. I therefore request the court recess until . . ."

"RECESSS DENIEDDDD . . ." came a haunting moan from the gallery.

Spock didn't let any distress he may have felt at this unanimous rejection show. "I shall have to make do with the testimony of witnesses, then." The Prosecutor showed no inclination to offer any aid.

"I call Lucien as my first witness."

A second flare of released energy and Lucien's

stocks, too, vanished. Spock moved to stand in front of him. "Lucien, of all the Megans, you alone do not seem to fear or hate humans. On the contrary, you appear to like them very much. Why?"

"Because I'm a glutton for punishment," the goatman replied, grinning. "No, this is not the time for levity, I suppose. I will try to be serious, though it's hard for me." He considered thoughtfully.

"I expect it's because they're so much like me, or I like them. Always questions to be answered! Like a child who continually questions his father, only to be asked, 'must there always be a reason for everything?' They are like that rare child who stares defiantly back up and says, 'yes!'

"I, too, am like that. And they have minds that never cease ranging outward, always seeking, striving to expand their store of knowledge . . . for knowledge's sake and not always for greed, as has been implied.

"It is these things that make them unique and endears them to me. But with us, it is different. Every Megan is always alone, always existing self-confident, assured, in a singular sphere of certainty, Whereas humans, for all their vaunted individuality, are a true gregarious society. It seems to be something I need, this group association."

He started to pace back and forth before the first row of benches, glancing occasionally upward and back into the higher balconies.

"As you know, I was among the first to go among them. In Mesopotamia, Ur, Babylonia, Greece. In the river valleys of the Hwang and the Indus, I saw these bonds developing between them. An easy companionship that Megas-tu has never known and, sadly, can never know.

"I meant to help and change them, and ended by having them change me." He turned to look at Spock. "That's why I adopted you when you arrived. It was another chance to recover something I'd . . . lost."

"Thank you, Lucien," said a satisfied Spock. "One other witness, if you please. Captain James T. Kirk."

Flare-dissolve, and Kirk's stocks became a comfortable wooden chair.

"Tell the court, Captain. Would you say that humans have not changed since the time of Salem?"

Kirk was startled at how easily the words came, how relaxed he was, considering the gravity of the situation. "I think that we've been trying to, Spock. A little at a time.

"The certain virtues of humanity, which Lucien has elaborated on so flatteringly, go hand in hand with our faults—greed, envy, fear. We've learned a great deal about ourselves in the centuries since the witch trials. We try to understand and respect each other, no matter what a man's peculiarities. We try to understand and respect all life forms.

"And the human race has adopted a motto, a standard that at the time of Salem was only a dream in the minds of a few enlightened men." His own voice rose.

"KNOWLEDGE IS FREEDOM".

"Indeed, Captain," Spock agreed, speaking quietly into the resultant silence. "Could you elaborate on these new standards of man?"

Kirk stood, faced the endless gallery. "The records of the *Enterprise* are open for your inspection, citizens of Megas-tu. We couldn't hide them from you or alter them now even if we wished to.

"All the history of Earth and its Federation of worlds is at your disposal. Look at it . . . look at general order number one: *No starship may interfere with the normal development of any alien life form or society, whether advanced or primitive!*

"Even requests for aid by dying primitives are often frowned upon, in the belief that interference from outside often does more harm than good. Compare that with the Earth you once knew. And you may also compare—"

"ENOUGH!" The voice of the Megan Prosecutor rumbled through the pastel pit of the hall. A sparkling, whirling cloud formed in the center of the gallery, breaking up into tiny cloud-fragments. These shrank to become the entire records section of the *Enterprise*.

It hovered there . . . tapes, computer inserts, kilometers of microfilm. A gust of wind rose and scattered the knowledge like leaves across the thousands of benches, tumbling in and around the intent Megans.

"HERE IS YOUR HISTORY, HERE ARE YOUR RECORDS . . . EXHIBIT A FOR THE DEFENSE!" The Prosecutor gestured yet again. The blowing tapes and cassettes vanished once more.

"YOU HAVE HEARD AND YOU HAVE SEEN AND YOU KNOW," the Prosecutor told the vast chamber. "CITIZENS . . . HOW DECIDE YOU?" He went silent, his attitude one of intense concentration.

Kirk and Spock and the others also strained to hear, but it was as still as the inside of a cave. Whatever discussion was taking place could not be detected by mere human senses.

Oddly, Kirk found himself musing on the fact, not that his life and the lives of his crew lay in the balance, but that he had not had anything to eat since Lucien's picnic. He was getting hungry.

The concerns of the human body are not philosophical in nature.

"A DECISION HAS BEEN MADE, CAPTAIN JAMES KIRK." He forgot about food and leaned forward.

"IT IS YOUR ASTROPHYSICS SECTION AND NOT THE HISTORICAL ONE THAT IS THE DECIDING FACTOR. ACCORDING TO THOSE RECORDS, YOUR ENTRY HERE TRULY WAS AN ACCIDENT OF EXPLORATION—AND ONE UNLIKELY TO BE SAFELY DUPLICATED.

"WITH THAT IN MIND, ADDED TO THE NEW EVIDENCE IN FAVOR OF MAN WHICH HAS BEEN PRESENTED, IT WOULD SEEM THAT WE OF MEGAS-TU ARE SAFE." He paused and his expression grew dark—literally.

"BUT LUCIEN MUST BE PUNISHED! FOR HIS BE-TRAYAL OF HIS PEOPLE AND THE DANGER HE HAS EXPOSED US TO. HE WHO WISHES COMPANIONSHIP SHALL BE CONFINED IN LIMBO FOR ALL ETERNITY!"

At those fateful final words a bubble of transparent red suddenly enveloped the goat-man. It pulsed softly with evidence of great power held under careful control. Without thinking, Kirk left his chair and rushed to the bubble's side.

"No—you can't. To isolate someone like Lucien—that's worse than sentencing him to death." The voice of the Prosecutor rose in volume and shrillness.

"DO YOU KNOW WHOM YOU DEFEND? DO YOU KNOW WHOSE COMFORT YOU SEEK? HE HAS TOLD YOU HIS NAME IS LUCIEN. WOULD YOU DEFEND HIM STILL IF YOU KNEW HIM BY ANOTHER NAME?

"INDEED IT WAS HE WHO WENT AMONG YOU AND SOUGHT YOUR FRIENDSHIP!" the voice laughed. "IN-DEED IT WAS HE WHO WORKED HIS MAGIC FOR YOU, IN HIS OWN WAYS. NO, IT SHALL NO LONGER BE.

"DOWN, LUCIFER!"

The goat-man leaned against the thin, impregnable walls of the bubble. Orange fire flared around his palms, terrible, all-destroying. But they could not break that shell. It started to rise.

Kirk's voice, when he had recovered from the initial shock of recognition and could speak again, was steady and determined.

"We're not interested in the remnants of legend and superstition, Prosecutor. I'd said we'd given such things up. He's a living, sentient being, an intelligent life-form, and he helped us. That's all I have to know about him. We'll not stand by and see him harmed for our past mistakes."

The Prosecutor gestured. A smoke-ring of blue energy appeared in the room and started to float toward Kirk. He twisted out of its way, and it changed direction like a thinking creature, pursuing him.

"SUBMIT TO THIS DECISION AND GO FREE, CAPTAIN. YOU HAVEN'T THE POWER TO FIGHT US."

"Captain!" urged Spock. "Use the magic you know." Kirk dodged around the base of the rising red bubble, the ring following. Suddenly, it looked as if he too were beginning to glow.

Little sparks and flashes of blue-green energy flickered and played around his body. Eyes a little drunk, he turned and gestured. A ball of green flame spun toward the Prosecutor.

A blazing fire appeared over him, feeding on nothing. It started to descend. Kirk made another gesture, shouted, "Powers of Earth and Sky, Appear! An extreme low pressure system has been detected moving north-northeast!"

Thunder boomed, miniature lightning crackled, and a howling rainstorm drenched the chamber, putting out the lowering fire.

There was a smattering of applause from the gallery.

The scene began to flutter and change constantly, like a dance viewed under intermittent strobe light, as Kirk and the Prosecutor exchanged gestures.

One moment they were standing in a street of Salem Town—then they were back on the naked surface of Megas-tu. A raging sandstorm swallowed them up.

"High humidity and dampness!" Kirk intoned reverently as the abrasive sand tore at him. "Deciduous foliage marked by high rainfall . . . !"

Desert turned to jungle. But the Prosecutor was already counter-gesturing, and the jungle melted into deep blue ocean, the tops of trees turning into wave crests.

Kirk choked as he took in a startled mouthful of sea water. He felt himself drowning.

"YOU CANNOT BEST AN ENTIRE WORLD, CAPTAIN KIRK. THERE IS NO WAY YOU CAN WIN."

"I have to!" he shouted, then choked again. "Don't you see, Prosecutor, you'll become as bad as the primitive humans you feared. A moment ago you said you'd never found it necessary to harm another being. But now you're going to do so, acting out a terror instead of the higher morals you always insisted you, and not we Earthmen, possessed!"

Floating high above the waves, the Prosecutor paused only a second before gesturing.

The world vanished.

Kirk found himself suddenly dry. The great hall was gone. He was back on the surface of the real Megas-tu. Colored particles and sand swirled harmlessly around him.

In the distance he could see the *Enterprise*, reassembled and whole. Behind him was the forest and the fairy city. The sand vanished, and he was standing on a green lawn with Spock and the Prosecutor. Lucien was there, too, still encased in the red bubble.

Even as he watched, the transparent prison began to dissolve.

"THE MOST MAGIC LIES ALWAYS IN YOUR HEART, HU-MAN," mused the Prosecutor, no longer a threatening figure. "YOU WERE PREPARED TO DIE FOR LUCIEN, A BEING WHO IS ALIEN TO YOU AND WHOSE RACIAL MEM-ORIES TO YOU ARE NOT THE BEST."

"I was sure you would do something at least as foolish, friend Kirk," the goat-man smiled. "It wouldn't have been human of you not to. I told them their fears of you were groundless. But they are so cautious now—not like us." For a being just threatened with limbo, he seemed remarkably cheerful.

"How could you be so certain the Captain would react the way he did?" asked a curious Spock.

There was a twinkle in Lucien's eye. "I know my humans. Their inconsistencies are the most predictable of all."

"I don't understand," began Kirk, but the Prosecutor smiled as he interrupted.

"THIS LAST WAS A TEST OF YOUR TRUE SELVES, CAP-

TAIN. HOW RIGHT YOU WERE WHEN YOU REMINDED ME OF OUR OWN WORDS, THAT WE COULD NOT INTENTIONALLY DO HARM TO OTHERS.

"WE HAD TO BE CERTAIN YOUR RECORDS WERE NO RUSE. THEY MIGHT HAVE BEEN DOCTORED BEFORE YOU ENTERED THE VORTEX. WE HAVE BEEN TRICKED TOO MANY TIMES TO TAKE CHANCES."

"I see now," nodded Spock. "You had to have incontrovertible proof that not only man's laws had changed, but that man himself had." He turned to Kirk. "Your compassion for Lucien was that proof, Captain."

"IF YOUR PEOPLE SHOULD CHANCE TO VISIT US AGAIN, CAPTAIN KIRK, WE SHALL DO OUR BEST TO WELCOME THEM. THE LIFTING OF THIS FEAR IS A GREAT THING. YOU HAVE GIVEN BACK TO US SOME OF WHAT YOUR ANCESTORS TOOK AWAY. WE SHALL PROVIDE YOU WITH THE EXTRADIMENSIONAL BOOST YOU WILL REQUIRE TO REENTER YOUR OWN UNIVERSE."

"And I'll give you something to make the changeover a little easier!" roared Lucien. He gestured, and tankards appeared in everyone's hand.

"A favorite archaic Earth custom of mine, Asmodeus. A toast—to a new friendship, and to the lifting of old fears." He tilted his head, raised his own huge container, and let the liquid run down his throat, chin, and beard.

Kirk did his best to imitate him, in spirit if not capacity. Spock sipped delicately at his own, and shook his head in wonder at the attractions of excessive alcoholic consumption ...

The universe was unchanged. Stars lay like gold flecks at the bottom of a prospector's pan, shining steadily through the lambent background of radiant nebulae.

Compared to this glory, the object that suddenly

burst into the central galactic quadrant from out of a peculiar confluence of force lines was unrelievedly dull.

To those who rode in it, however, this miniscule symmetrical blot—*the Enterprise*—was a more perfect jewel than the greatest star.

As before, the central viewscreen on the bridge could capture only a small section of the glowing panorama.

"Report, Mr. Scott," said Kirk crisply, leaning over to speak into the pickup grid in the command chair arm. The chief engineer's voice responded from another part of the starship.

"All systems operative, Captain. Warp-engines performing perfectly. Everything's operatin' at maximum efficiency again. It wasn't too hard." There was a pause. "I only had to sacrifice a chicken and two goats to the central computer."

"Very funny, Scotty," Kirk said dryly as the chief's chortle floated back over the intercom. He switched it off in mid-chortle.

"No more magic for us, Jim," a relieved McCoy declared from Kirk's side. He gestured at the screen. "It's all back there, and there it can stay, for all I care. Though I won't be so quick to laugh at any alien witch doctors we may meet up with in the future."

For awhile they simply enjoyed the retreating magnificence of the galactic center, a torrent of raw, untappable energy. It seemed it existed only for their visual pleasure, now.

"I'm not a particularly religious man, Jim," McCoy murmured after several minutes of contemplative consideration of the vast spectacle, "but do you think that Lucien was really the ancient devil-demon some men called Lucifer? Or was it all an act, a guise he liked to assume for his own amusement?"

"You mean," Kirk asked, "did Lucien pattern himself after the myth, or did the myth arise out of Lucien? I don't know, Bones. Does it matter?"

"Oh, I suppose not." McCoy was quiet for a few minutes more, before speaking idly again.

"It's just that—if he was, Jim—this would be the second time he was on the verge of being cast out. But thanks to you, this is the first time he was saved."

Kirk looked sharply back at McCoy. There was no sign of a smile on the doctor's face. He started to say something, caught himself, and returned his attention to the viewscreen instead. He had other things to think about.

They had a long way to go.